THE CASE: Five years ago singer Curtis Taylor died on a lonely highway—and Nancy's convinced that the accident was no accident.

CONTACT: Louisa Hunt, a friend of Bess and George, claims she saw Taylor's ghost; all Nancy sees is an unsolved murder.

SUSPECTS: Melanie Taylor—*the singer's widow had little to mourn about when she inherited his vast estate.*

J. J. Rahmer—*Taylor's former manager didn't inherit any money, just the affection of the dead man's wife.*

Spike Wilson—*Curtis Taylor fired the drummer from his band . . . and a week later Taylor was history.*

COMPLICATIONS: Five years is a long time—certainly time enough to cover up any evidence of murder.

Books in The Nancy Drew Files® Series

Available from ARCHWAY Paperbacks

THE NANCY DREW FILES™

Case 65
FINAL NOTES

CAROLYN KEENE

AN ARCHWAY PAPERBACK
Published by POCKET BOOKS
New York   London   Toronto   Sydney   Tokyo   Singapore

AN ARCHWAY PAPERBACK *Original*

An Archway Paperback published by
POCKET BOOKS, a division of Simon & Schuster Inc.
1230 Avenue of the Americas, New York, NY 10020

Copyright © 1991 by Simon & Schuster Inc.
Produced by Mega-Books of New York, Inc.

ISBN: 0-671-73069-X

First Archway Paperback printing November 1991

10 9 8 7 6 5 4 3 2 1

Cover art by Tom Galasinski

Printed in the U.S.A.

IL 6+

FINAL NOTES

Chapter

One

COME ON, Nancy," Bess Marvin urged, leaning forward from the back seat of Nancy Drew's blue Mustang. "I know you can drive faster than this."

Nancy caught her friend's pleading blue eyes in the rearview mirror. "Sure I can, Bess," she said. "But there's this thing called a speed limit, remember?"

"But I can't wait to get there," Bess insisted. "It isn't every day we go to the hometown of the greatest country singer who ever lived."

Bess's cousin George Fayne turned in the passenger seat to grin at Bess. "Think how much more you'll enjoy the experience if you get there alive," George teased. Reaching for the cassette case next to her, she added, "Maybe music would help you pass the time until we get to Maywood. How about some Curtis Taylor?"

"Good idea," Bess said. "I mean, we *are* going to the five-year memorial gala commemorating his death. Put on 'Losing My Heart.'"

George gave her cousin a dubious look. "Are you sure, Bess? We've heard it about a hundred times already."

"You can't hear a great song too many times, George," Bess answered. "It's impossible."

Laughing, George popped a cassette into Nancy's deck. Soon the rough, masculine voice of Curtis Taylor filled the car.

"I didn't mean to lose my heart," he sang. "It just happened that way. . . ."

Bess joined in: "But now I'm lost in the feeling, and it won't go away. . . ."

"Oh, darlin', oh, darlin'," George broke out singing with Curtis and Bess, "let's make this moment stay . . ."

"'Cause I'm losing my heart to you," Nancy chimed in.

"He sure could sing," George said when the song was over. She picked up one of the cassettes and admired Curtis Taylor's smiling photo on the cover. "Gorgeous, too. All that black hair . . ."

"And those devastating ice-blue eyes," Bess added with a sigh.

Nancy glanced at her two friends. Dark-haired, athletic George and petite, blond Bess had completely different looks and interests. But one thing they both shared was an appreciation of cute guys.

"What a loss," Nancy murmured. "Think of all the music Curtis Taylor could have created in the past five years if he were still around."

"Well, maybe he is, Nancy," George said with a wry smile. "I mean, Aunt Louisa swears she saw Curtis alive and well just yesterday outside the Maywood Civic Center, where the concert is being held."

Aunt Louisa, Nancy knew, was not really Bess and George's aunt, but a close friend of their parents. For years Bess and George had been telling Nancy what a big Curtis Taylor fan Louisa Hunt was. Louisa had driven all over the country to see Curtis Taylor concerts when he was still alive. She'd even moved to the star's home base in Maywood, which was a two-hour drive from the girls' hometown, River Heights, in Illinois.

"Have you seen the headlines recently in the *Weekly Scoop*?" George continued "'Curtis Taylor Seen Alive.' 'Curtis Taylor to Return for Big Concert.'"

"Maybe we'll get lucky and see him ourselves!" Bess bubbled.

Nancy had to laugh. "Yeah, right," she said. "Maybe we'll see the Martians land, while we're at it. Didn't the *Scoop* say something about that, too?"

Bess didn't seem at all daunted by Nancy's comment. "Well, if there's anyone who can find out for sure whether Curtis Taylor is still alive, it's you, Nan. That's why we told Aunt Louisa we'd come four days before Saturday's concert. After all, not everyone is friends with a great detective."

"I'm flattered," Nancy said with a grin. "But I generally hunt criminals, not ghosts."

"Who said anything about ghosts?" Bess said. "We're talking about Curtis's disappearing and then coming back. Maybe he just needed a break from the pressures of stardom or something."

"A five-year break?" Nancy asked, rolling her blue eyes and pushing a lock of reddish blond hair back from her face. "It's more likely that Louisa has an overactive imagination when it comes to her idol. Don't get me wrong," Nancy added. "I mean, we were planning to go to the gala anyway, and it was really nice of Louisa to get us the tickets. I'm happy to check this out for you.

"They say Curtis's widow is a really hot singer," Nancy said, changing the subject.

"Melanie Taylor? Yeah, she's okay, I guess," Bess said indifferently. "But Curtis's nephew Tyrone Taylor is the one I want to see. What a hunk!"

"Tyrone?" Nancy echoed. "I don't think I've ever heard of him."

"You and practically everyone else," George said wryly. "He's not very well known."

Shooting her cousin an indignant look, Bess said, "Well, he ought to be. George, pull out the purple cassette that says *Heartthrob*. That's him on the cover."

When George showed her the cassette, Nancy saw that Tyrone Taylor had the same glossy black hair as his uncle, but had more delicate features, with piercing green eyes and a cocky grin.

"He's cute, all right," Nancy said, bobbing her head to the music as Curtis Taylor broke into "Loose as a Goose."

"Ohhh, I'm loose as a goose, as a goose on the loose. I was caught in a noose, but youuuu . . . you set me freeeeee . . ." sang the masculine voice.

"I love this one," Nancy confessed with a giggle. "Some of Curtis's old band members are performing in the concert Saturday, too, right?"

George nodded, running a hand through her short brown curls. "Yeah, most of them have gone solo," she informed Nancy. "All except for Spike Wilson, the drummer. He doesn't play anymore. He was in an accident or something. Oh, and the Blue Mountain Boys are going to be there, too, doing a special tribute to Curtis."

"Oooo, I'm excited," Bess added with a little shiver. "This concert is going to be great."

Seeing the exit for Maywood, Nancy turned her car off the highway. A big sign at the front of the exit ramp read Welcome to Maywood—Home of the One and Only Curtis Taylor. Another sign tacked up beneath it read Fifth Anniversary Memorial Gala Saturday, November 10, 8:00 P.M. Stenciled over that sign in red letters were the words Sold Out.

Following her friends' directions, Nancy drove along the town's main street. They passed billboard after billboard offering tributes to the late, great star. Then they turned onto a tree-lined street and soon pulled into the driveway of a split-level house.

"This is it," Bess said, getting out of the car with her overnight bag slung over her shoulder. Nancy and George got their things from the trunk, then joined Bess, who was ringing the doorbell. While they waited, Nancy enjoyed the crisp fall air and stretched out her long, slender legs.

A woman with graying blond hair, large eyeglasses, and hazel eyes opened the door, and Bess cried enthusiastically, "Aunt Louisa!"

Nancy knew that Louisa had to be in her late forties, but she looked much younger. Her hair was pulled back in a ponytail, and she wore snug-fitting blue jeans and running shoes.

"Bess and George—you both look fabulous," Louisa said, hugging both girls and beaming as she ushered them into the house. "And you must be Nancy. Thanks so much for coming.

"Make yourselves at home," Louisa said, gesturing toward the living room just beyond the front hall. Nancy saw that it was a very comfortable, if disorganized, room with a variety of couches, chairs, lamps, and throw pillows that looked as if they had been acquired at random over the years. "I'll show you up to your rooms later. Let's just relax for a while."

Nancy dropped her bag next to her friends' things in the front hall and walked over to a group of pictures hanging above a dark blue sofa in the living room. They were mostly Curtis Taylor concert posters and album covers, including an autographed photo of the musician, inscribed "Best Wishes to Louisa Hunt." Next to it was an eight-by-ten glossy photo of several women standing in a line with the star himself.

"That's you," Nancy said, pointing to a younger-looking Louisa in the picture.

"Yes, it is," Louisa said proudly. Walking over to Nancy, she pushed her glasses back up to get a better look. "It was taken many years ago at a fan club convention. That's the only time I ever met Curtis in person. Of course, it was only for a minute."

Louisa let out a big sigh and continued. "He was just the greatest. Very warm and very sweet. And to think that we may have him back again. It's just so thrilling." She sighed again, then said, "Can I get you girls some lemonade?"

Obviously, Louisa isn't going to give up on her belief that Curtis Taylor is alive, Nancy thought, until I prove her wrong. And this is as good a time as any to start on my case. Nancy followed Louisa and her friends into the country-style kitchen.

A few minutes later, when they were all settled around the table sipping their lemonade, Nancy turned to Louisa and asked, "Did anyone else see Curtis Taylor yesterday when you did?"

Louisa's face grew serious. "Not that I know of," she answered. "I managed to get this week off from my teaching job, so I was in the parking lot of the Civic Center—you know, just keeping an eye out for anyone famous. With all the crowds coming to town, I wanted to be there extra early. So I bought a copy of the *Scoop* and a cup of coffee, and I was reading in the car. Then, all of a sudden, I looked up, and there he was. I'll show you the place tomorrow, if you want."

"How close was he to your car?" Nancy probed.

"Oh, a couple of hundred feet, I guess. He was coming out of the building's rear entrance. But I saw him as plain as day. Unfortunately, it was only for a second. By the time I got my other glasses on, he was gone."

Shooting a quizzical look at Louisa, George asked, "Your other glasses?"

Louisa nodded. "The ones I wear for distance. I had my reading glasses on at first," she explained.

"Then how do you know it was him, Aunt Louisa?" Bess asked, biting her lip. "Maybe you just saw someone who looked like Curtis Taylor."

For a second Louisa looked hurt, then a soft smile spread across her face, and she said dreamily, "Oh, it was him all right, Bess. I'd know that face anywhere. He looked as handsome as the time he was first on television, on 'The Red Reilly Show.' Did I ever tell you about that, how Curtis got his big break? You know, he was just a country boy from Harlow County back then, and . . ."

Nancy glanced over at Bess and George. They were both completely wrapped up in Louisa's tale, which began at the start of Curtis's career and continued all the way to the day Louisa heard about his death. By that time the older woman's eyes were filled with tears.

"I was just devastated when I got the news about the car crash. And I never dreamed I'd see him again. Oh, aren't we lucky, all of us, to have such a great artist back again!"

The look on Louisa's face was sheer rapture. She was a very sweet person, Nancy thought. Still, Nancy couldn't help wondering exactly what she had gotten herself into this time.

"Wow. Traffic's pretty heavy," Nancy commented the next morning as she, Louisa, Bess, and George rode in Nancy's car toward the Civic Center. Nancy wanted to see for herself the spot where Louisa had supposedly seen Curtis Taylor.

"There are fifty thousand people expected in town this weekend," Louisa told the girls. "I don't know where they're going to put them all." She pointed up ahead to an oval-shaped modern building made of concrete and tinted glass. "There's the Civic Center. Go in the first entrance and park to the right."

Although the concert wasn't for another three days, the parking lot was crowded, and there were swarms of people outside the enormous concrete area that marked the Civic Center entrance. Still, Nancy managed to find a spot where Louisa directed her, around the side of the building.

"I was parked right near here," Louisa said. She leaned forward excitedly in the passenger seat and pointed. "And I saw him over there, by the stage door."

Spotting the inconspicuous set of double doors near the Civic Center's rear, Nancy suggested, "Let's get out and take a look."

"Brrr, it's cold," Bess said, climbing out of the backseat after George and zipping up her leather jacket. George and Louisa stepped out, too, shading their eyes against the morning sun.

They were about halfway to the double doors when Louisa stopped suddenly and murmured, "Oh, my. Oh, I don't believe this. Look over there!"

Nancy's eyes followed Louisa's pointing finger, and she froze in shocked amazement. There, by a doorway, was a man with black hair and blue eyes, wearing a white suit with sequins on the lapels.

"He looks exactly like his picture on Bess's cassette cover," George murmured. "It's Curtis Taylor himself!"

Chapter

Two

"I**T** *IS* HIM," Bess said shakily. "I don't believe it."

Nancy was still staring at the man when George touched her lightly on the arm. "Look behind him, Nan," George said with a gulp. Nancy's mouth fell open as *another* Curtis Taylor stepped out of the doorway, wearing an identical white suit.

"What in the world—?" she murmured.

"There's another one!" Bess exclaimed as a third Curtis came out and joined the other two.

That does it, Nancy thought. There's no way three Curtis Taylors have come back from the dead. "Come on," she said, stepping forward purposefully. "Let's find out what this is all about."

Half walking, half running, the four women hurried across the lot.

"Is one of you Curtis Taylor?" Bess blurted out as soon as they came up to the three.

The men looked at Bess, then at each other, then burst out laughing.

The stage doors opened once more, and another man stepped out. He had black hair and green eyes and was informally dressed in jeans, with a black T-shirt and a denim jacket. "Here's the guy who can give you some answers," one of the Curtis Taylors said.

"Tyrone Taylor!" Bess exclaimed, awestruck. "I think *Heartthrob* is a brilliant album. You're totally fantastic."

The young singer looked surprised and pleased. "Well, well, thank you," he said. "Isn't this a nice way to start off the day?"

One of the white-suited men flicked a thumb at Nancy and her friends, saying, "We threw these ladies for a loop, Ty. They thought we were Curtis."

"These men are professional impersonators," Tyrone explained to the girls, chuckling. "We're thinking of using them at the gala. And if you think they look like my uncle, you should hear them sing. It's spooky."

"I guess I saw one of you a couple days ago," Louisa said, looking slightly stunned. "I could have sworn it was Curtis, too."

George put a comforting arm around Louisa while Tyrone turned to the three impersonators and said, "Fellas, give me some time to think it over, okay? I'll be in touch this afternoon."

"Sorry if we gave you girls a scare," one of the men said.

"Well," Nancy said, watching them go, "that certainly clears up the mystery. By the way," she added, holding out her hand to Tyrone Taylor, "I'm Nancy Drew. And these are my friends Bess Marvin, George Fayne, and Louisa Hunt."

Bess started rummaging through her handbag. "I know everyone must ask you this all the time," she said to Tyrone, "but could you please sign an autograph?" Giving him her most appealing smile, she held out a pen and a crumpled store receipt. "This is the only paper I have on me."

Tyrone returned Bess's smile, and Nancy noted again that he seemed pleased at the recognition. "I think I can do better than that," he said. "How would you ladies like to come with me to Greenwood? I have a few photos there that I can sign, and while we're at it, we can have a quick lunch."

"At Curtis Taylor's estate? You've got to be

kidding!" George exclaimed, exchanging an excited look with Louisa.

"That sounds great," Bess added, turning to her friends. Her face was lit up with a gigantic grin.

Wow, thought Nancy, George must have been right when she said that Tyrone was an unknown. Most famous musicians would never have been so friendly.

"Well, actually, the estate belongs to Melanie and me, now that Uncle Curtis is gone. Seeing as you're the first person who ever asked me for my autograph," Tyrone said with a laugh, "I'd say it's the least I can do. Come on. My car's over here."

As the others started to follow the handsome singer to the stretch limousine parked at the curb, Nancy said, "I'll follow in my car. Wait for me to catch up, okay?"

"I'll go with Nancy to keep her company," George said, turning and jogging back to Nancy.

The two girls hurried to Nancy's car. "Is this unbelievable or what?" George said, climbing in.

"It's fantastic," Nancy agreed with a laugh. "At this rate I could really learn to be a fan."

The ride out to the Taylor mansion didn't take long. Within twenty minutes Nancy and George had reached the main entrance to Greenwood, which was lined with tour buses.

Following the limousine, Nancy bypassed the crowded stone gateway and pulled up to a set of tall, old-fashioned iron gates, several hundred yards farther down the drive.

Nancy saw Tyrone exchange a few words with the security guard at the gate and point back to her car. A moment later the guard waved Nancy through with a friendly smile.

"Hey, V.I.P. treatment," Nancy said, grinning at George. "I could get used to this."

The mansion was some distance off, peeking from behind oak and evergreen trees at the top of a knoll. There was a stone wall running along the knoll, slightly downhill from the house, and as Nancy drove closer, she could see over the barrier. There were hordes of tourists on the other side of the wall, but apparently the part of the estate Nancy was in, including the mansion, was private.

"Oh, I see the tombstone," George said, looking out her side of the car. "I recognize it from a million pictures."

Craning her neck, Nancy took a look. The tombstone, on the part of the estate open to the public, was an ornately carved block of granite next to a stone sculpture in the shape of a guitar. "So many people," she murmured. "And look at all those buildings the fans are going in and out of. Millions of fans must pour through here every year."

As Nancy followed Tyrone's limo past a

small stand of pine trees, the mansion came into view. It was an immense, stately stone structure, with pillars and a slate roof.

"Whoa," George murmured. "Talk about awesome."

"How'd you like to come home to this every day?" Nancy joked. She pulled to a stop next to Tyrone's limousine, and she and George got out of the car.

"Welcome to my home sweet home," Tyrone said. "This way in." He gallantly held his arm out, motioning for them to walk ahead.

"Oh, Nancy," Bess whispered as they walked toward the entrance. "Isn't this the most incredible thing that's ever happened to you? Tyrone is so sweet. I mean, he's an entertainer, but he's so down to earth and funny."

Nancy arched a brow at George, who grinned and said, "Sounds like she's got a crush, Nan."

"You guys!" Bess protested, blushing.

Just then the door swung open in front of them, held by a butler with slicked-back gray hair, wearing a dark green uniform with polished brass buttons. "Hi there, Vickers!" Tyrone called out.

"Good day, sir," the butler said levelly.

"Vickers runs this place practically single-handed," Tyrone explained. "He's been here forever."

From behind the servant a tall, thin man with long, straight brown hair, brown eyes, and a small silver earring stepped out.

"Hi, Spike," Tyrone said, smiling.

Spike nodded briefly at Tyrone but ignored Nancy, Bess, George, and Louisa as he walked off across the lawn, toward a nearby gazebo.

"That's Spike Wilson," Louisa murmured.

"You mean Curtis's drummer?" George inquired.

Tyrone nodded. "He doesn't play anymore, not since he smashed his wrist in that car accident. Now he works here helping to manage Greenwood—you know, calling the plumber, filling in when the gardener goes on vacation, stuff like that. Melanie felt sorry for him, I guess, so she gave him a job. She's got a warm heart, my aunt does." Nancy thought she detected a note of sarcasm in Tyrone's voice, but she wasn't sure.

"Oh, Nancy!" Bess gasped as they stepped inside. "Isn't this fabulous?"

Nancy had to agree. And from the wonder in George's and Louisa's eyes, Nancy could tell they were awestruck, too. The front hall had a black-and-white checkered marble floor, a huge bouquet of fresh flowers on a carved pedestal, a crystal chandelier, and beautiful pale pink silk covering the walls. The wide hallway seemed to stretch almost endlessly to the sweeping marble staircase that curved toward the second level.

"I must have been to Greenwood a thousand times, but I never thought I'd get to see the private part of the estate," Louisa gushed. "I've seen it in so many photos. There's a famous picture of Curtis and Melanie standing on these steps the day they were married."

"Speaking of the lovely Melanie . . ." Tyrone said, his eyes glancing up the stairs. This time there was no mistaking the sarcasm in his voice.

Nancy followed his gaze and saw a beautiful blond woman descending the stairs. She was informally dressed in a pair of white leggings and an oversize T-shirt with padded shoulders and a beaded design on the front. Nonetheless, Melanie Taylor carried herself with dignity and grace. The only thing out of place in her picture-perfect looks was the angry scowl on her face.

"You didn't tell me you were bringing guests into my home," Melanie snapped at Tyrone. "It's bad enough I have to put up with thousands of strangers on the grounds every day. I refuse to turn my house into a museum for the morbidly curious, too. I need my privacy." With that she stormed back up the stairs.

Tyrone turned to the girls with an uncomfortable smile. "Please don't take what she

19

said personally. Aunt Melanie is a little tense about the upcoming concert, that's all." Clapping his hands together, he said, "Now, why don't I give you a quick tour before lunch?"

"That Melanie's a real witch," Louisa whispered to Nancy as Bess and George walked ahead with Tyrone down a long hallway lined with gold and platinum records in frames. "She just can't stand it that Curtis left half his estate to Tyrone. But Tyrone can bring in anyone he wants to. The biggest mistake of Curtis's life was marrying Melanie."

Melanie hadn't exactly been welcoming, but in Nancy's book that didn't make her a witch. Nancy couldn't help wondering if Louisa's remarks were prompted by jealousy. She would probably disapprove of any woman Curtis Taylor married.

Tyrone showed them the formal living room first. "Please be careful not to disturb anything here," he told the girls, gesturing to the room's beautiful furniture, marble fireplace, and elegant wooden bar. "Everything's been left exactly as it was the night Uncle Curtis passed on." He shrugged, explaining, "That's for the benefit of some historical group that's allowed in for a tour once every year."

Then Tyrone led them down another hallway, where he stopped in front of a set of double doors. "This was Uncle Curtis's studio suite," Tyrone said, throwing open the doors. "He created all his music here. At Melanie's request, everything has been left exactly as it was the night he passed on. Please be careful not to disturb anything."

The girls and Louisa went through the doors. Inside was a large study, with a desk, some shelves, and leather sofas and recliners. A movie screen, a large shelf of cataloged records, and more framed awards hung from the walls. Through an interior window they saw the studio itself.

"What's behind that door?" Nancy asked, pointing to a door next to the movie screen.

"That was Uncle Curtis's closet," Tyrone explained. "He kept his costumes there."

Bess spun around, taking it all in. "Here we are in Curtis Taylor's private studio," she said. "Unbelievable!"

Walking over to the costume closet, Tyrone said, "As long as we're here, maybe you ladies could help me out with something. I have a costume check back at the Civic Center this afternoon, and I haven't even decided what to wear yet."

Tyrone pulled out a key, then unlocked the door and led them inside.

"Uncle Curtis left me all of his costumes," the young singer explained as he fingered one and then another. With all their sequins and spangles, the different-colored outfits made a dazzling display. "His dream was that I'd follow in his footsteps as a performer."

Bess looked around in awe. "Wow," she said. "This closet is bigger than my whole bedroom."

Smiling at Bess, Tyrone said, "Uncle Curtis did have a lot of costumes. This will be the first time I've worn one, though. I guess I feel a little funny wearing his clothes. He was like a father to me," he added, his voice growing husky.

He shook his head in amazement. "I guess that's one reason I'm not sure about those impersonators. They give me the creeps."

"You mean, you haven't hired them yet?" George asked.

"Not yet," Tyrone said, looking concerned. "There's another reason, too. This concert could be my big break, but if everybody's talking about the Curtis look-alikes . . ."

Nancy nodded. "I see what you mean," she said. "Then you wouldn't get much exposure."

"Hey," said Bess, who'd been looking through the clothes. "This would look dynamite on you." She held up a gold lamé cowboy suit. "It would set off your black hair and green eyes just great," she added, her cheeks turning red.

Taking the suit from her, Tyrone held it up to a mirror to look at it. "I wonder how the jacket will fit," he said, frowning at his reflection. "Uncle Curtis was a little more muscular than I am."

Tyrone put on the jacket and faced the mirror again. "Fits perfectly. Good choice, Bess," he said. "Except . . ." He frowned, patting a thick lump in the jacket's right pocket.

"Hey, what's this?" he murmured, pulling a thick envelope from the pocket. "It's addressed to Philip Hayward. That's my uncle's lawyer," he explained. "And it's in Uncle Curtis's handwriting. Maybe I should take a peek."

He opened the envelope and took out a cassette tape, a folded-over piece of paper with musical notations on it, and a note written in script.

" 'Dear Philip,' " Tyrone read, " 'in the event of anything happening to me suddenly and unexpectedly, please give the contents of this envelope to my nephew, Tyrone.' "

Sighing, Tyrone said, "It's signed 'Curtis.' "

Nancy looked over Tyrone's shoulder as he unfolded the second sheet, which consisted of musical notations and a lyric written out in block print.

"It's a song called 'Melanie,' " Tyrone announced, after looking quickly at it. "I'll bet this is what's on the cassette. Let's have a listen."

Tyrone led them back into the studio, where

he popped the tape into a cassette player that sat on top of a large control board.

But as the sound came on, it quickly became clear that the tape wasn't a recording of a song at all. Instead, Curtis Taylor's unmistakably rough voice filled the room, speaking in a hushed, worried tone: "Tyrone, somebody's out to kill me. Please believe me, because I'm as certain of this as I am of anything. In case anything happens to me, I want you to know who the person is. It's—"

On the tape there came the sudden sound of someone knocking, as a clock struck eight. "Coming," said Curtis's voice.

And that was all. They let the tape run, but there was nothing else. Nancy felt an ominous sensation in the pit of her stomach, and she exchanged an uncomfortable look with her friends.

"I guess he never got to finish it," Louisa said hesitantly.

"Unless . . ." Tyrone's face went white, and his hand flew to his cheek. "Does this mean the car crash wasn't an accident? Could it be that Uncle Curtis was *murdered?*"

Chapter

Three

I'VE GOT TO HEAR that tape again," Tyrone said, quickly pressing the rewind button. The dead man's message came on, and Nancy and her friends all listened to it intently once more.

Curtis spoke in the same hushed, desperate tone. ". . . who the person is. It's—" As the clock on the tape struck eight, Nancy glanced around the studio and looked through the interior window to the study. Spotting an antique wooden clock on the wall, she walked over to it and advanced the hands to the next hour—noon. The chime was identical to the one on the tape. After resetting the clock, Nancy rejoined the others.

"That cassette was recorded right here in

this studio," Nancy said. "When the knock came, Curtis must have gone into his dressing closet and hidden the tape, along with the other stuff you found."

Tyrone gave Nancy a quizzical look. "Why wouldn't he just put it in whatever he was wearing?"

Nancy shrugged. "You saw what a big bulge the envelope made in his pocket. Maybe he didn't want anyone to find it, including the person who knocked on the door. So he put it where he could find it later."

"Except he never got to it," George finished with a shiver.

Nancy gave Tyrone and her friends a meaningful look. "My guess would be that he died before he had a chance to. Tyrone, I think it would be best if you didn't say anything about this to anyone yet. The person who wanted to kill Curtis could be someone you know."

Tyrone nodded soberly.

Louisa, who had been standing rigid and silent for all of this, suddenly began shaking. "According to all the articles, Curtis died not long after eight, the time in the tape," she whispered. "Maybe someone killed him right after he taped that. Oh, this is too horrible."

"Tyrone, could you play the song for us?" Nancy suggested. "Since it was with the letter, it could be a clue. Maybe it'll tell us something."

He quickly moved to the electronic keyboard next to the tape deck. "Why didn't I think of that?"

"Nancy's a detective, Tyrone," Bess told him. "A really good one."

Giving Nancy a shaky smile, Tyrone said, "Well, isn't that lucky for me. Maybe you'll be able to help me figure all this out."

"I'd be happy to," Nancy said. "Mind if I hold on to that note for a little while?"

"Just take good care of it," Tyrone said, handing her the letter his uncle had written to the lawyer and the envelope it had come in.

"Don't worry, I will," Nancy said.

Spreading the music sheet out flat in front of him, Tyrone poised his fingers on the keys, ready to play. But before he could begin, there was a knock at the door.

Louisa went over and opened it. Spike Wilson stood in the doorway with a cordless telephone in his hand. "Ty, Platinum Entertainment is on the phone," he said. "They say it's urgent." Giving Nancy and her friends a curious look, Spike handed the phone to the young singer, then walked out of the studio.

Tyrone put his ear to the phone and said hello, then listened with a look of annoyance on his face. "Okay, I'll be there," he said into the receiver. "I said I'll be there!" Then he put down the phone and turned to the girls.

"I'm sorry, but we'll have to cancel lunch.

I've got to get to the Civic Center right away," he told them all. "They've moved up the time of the costume check, and then there's going to be a party for the bands and the press."

Bess's blue eyes lit up. "A party? That sounds so exciting."

Shooting Bess a big smile, Tyrone said, "You're all invited, of course."

"Great. Let's go," George urged.

"Okay," Louisa agreed quietly. Her mood had definitely been affected by hearing Curtis Taylor's voice on the tape, Nancy noticed.

"I'll check the song out later, when I have time to concentrate on it," Tyrone said, folding the sheet of music and sticking it in his jeans pocket. Then he took off the gold lamé jacket and put it on the hanger with the rest of the suit. "Come on. We're out of here."

Nancy tapped her foot to the music as a four-piece band played country rock in the second-floor banquet room Tyrone had led the girls to at the Civic Center. Seeing Bess dancing with Tyrone, and George dancing with a tall blond-haired guy, Nancy missed her long-time boyfriend, Ned Nickerson. Louisa seemed subdued, she noticed. Nancy couldn't get into a party mood, either—she just kept thinking about the tape.

"Louisa, do you know if Curtis Taylor had

any enemies?" Nancy asked, pouring a glass of punch.

Louisa bit her lip and shook her head helplessly. "Until this morning I thought I knew everything there was to know about Curtis Taylor. But never in a million years would I have suspected that someone would try to kill him."

"What happened on the day he died?" Nancy probed. "You must have read all the papers."

"Oh, I did. Every one of them," Louisa told her. "The accident happened just before nine o'clock outside Maywood, on Route four-fifty-nine. According to what I read, nobody knew where he was going. He had been home most of the day with Melanie. They had dinner together, and then at around eight-thirty he went out."

After taking a sip of her punch, Nancy asked, "Did he say why?"

Louisa shrugged. "Melanie said that he told her he had to go meet someone, but he didn't say who. They found his car the next morning, in a gully near Maywood Creek. It had gone off the road and struck the bank of a ditch. The coroner took Melanie to identify the body. They say Curtis was killed instantly."

Removing her glasses, Louisa dabbed at her eyes with a tissue and went on. "There was a huge funeral, attended by thousands of grieving fans, including me, of course. The casket was closed, which is why some people say he never really died, I suppose." She smiled sheepishly. "Until today, *I* wasn't sure he was really gone."

Nancy quickly went over in her mind what Louisa had just told her. "So according to the articles, nobody saw him dead except for the police, the coroner, and Melanie?"

"I guess," Louisa said.

The circumstances of Curtis Taylor's death seemed fairly routine, Nancy thought. On the other hand, the message the singer had left the night he died was anything but routine.

"Why aren't you two dancing?" Bess asked, coming over to Nancy and Louisa. "There are tons of cute guys here."

"And they're all twenty years too young for me," Louisa put in, chuckling for the first time all afternoon.

Nancy gestured toward where George was still dancing. "Who's that blond guy with George?" she asked Bess.

"His name is Eddie," Bess told her. "He's really sweet. He's an assistant director here at the Civic Center."

"Where's Tyrone?" Louisa asked.

Bess frowned and nodded her head to the left. Without turning to look, she said, "He's over there giving an interview." Nancy glanced in the direction Bess indicated and saw Tyrone talking to a pretty, dark-haired girl.

Giving Bess a reassuring pat on the shoulder, Nancy said, "She's probably just some reporter. He has to talk to those people for publicity."

"Thanks for saying that, Nan. I hope it's true," Bess said, brightening a little. "Oh, look, there's Malcolm Coleman." She nodded toward the suite's door. "He was Curtis's bass player."

Louisa whipped her head around, then said, "And that's Billy Rutteridge walking behind him. He played keyboards for Curtis in the old days, before he became a solo artist."

Seeing Curtis Taylor's old band members, Nancy got an idea. "Do me a favor, will you, you two?" Nancy asked Bess and Louisa. "Talk to them. See what you can find out about Curtis and who he might have gone to meet the night he died. I'll meet you guys at Louisa's for dinner, okay?"

Bess gave Nancy a quizzical look. "Where are you going?"

"There are a few things I want to find out. I'll tell you all about it later, okay?" Before they could answer, Nancy was halfway across the floor and then out the door. She stopped in the lobby just long enough to look up the address of the Maywood police department and buy a local map from the convenience store in the lobby.

Twenty minutes later Nancy was standing in the coroner's office, talking to a woman behind the front desk.

"Hi, I'm from the *River Heights Morning Enquirer*," Nancy fibbed. "We're doing a report on Curtis Taylor's death, and I was wondering if I could take a peek at the report that was filed when he died."

The secretary looked at Nancy, then shook her head and mumbled under her breath, "I wish I had a dollar for every person who's asked to see that report this week. Wait here and I'll get it."

The woman ambled through a door at the rear of the reception area, then returned a few minutes later with a one-page report, which she handed to Nancy. "Here it is, for what it's worth."

Nancy's practiced eyes went right to the crucial section: "Subject died as a result of head and chest injuries sustained in a one-vehicle accident, around 8:45 P.M. Blood alcohol content insignificant at .03 percent, equivalent to one drink. Subject's wife confirms he had one drink, his habitual nightly bourbon, at 8:00 P.M. This information conforms to our office's findings. We conclude blood alcohol content did not contribute to subject's death. Car was found to be without defect. Brakes were in working order. Conclusion: Death was accidental and instantaneous."

The report was signed by someone named Dexter Mobley. "Is Mr. Mobley in?" Nancy asked after she'd handed the paper back to the secretary.

"Oh, no. He retired. Soon after Curtis Taylor died, in fact," the receptionist told Nancy.

Nancy frowned. "Does he live in town?"

The other woman shook her head. "He's in a nursing home called Windemere House. It's up on Overview Terrace."

"Thanks," Nancy told her with a smile. "You've been very helpful."

With a shrug the secretary returned to her desk. "I don't know why you newspeople can't leave well enough alone," she muttered.

Nancy went back outside and got in her car. It was growing dark, and in the deepening shadows she mulled over the report she'd just read. It had left her disturbed and confused. It was incredibly short and uninformative, especially considering the fame of its subject.

What now? Curtis's accident had taken place on Route 459, Nancy remembered from her conversation with Louisa. Near some stream—Maywood Creek, that was it. Flicking on the overhead light, Nancy consulted her map, then drove to the site.

As cars whizzed by, she pulled over next to the guardrail and parked, putting on her emergency flashers. There, off to the right, the gully where Curtis Taylor had met his untimely death was a pitch-black wedge between the grayer shadows of the surrounding slopes. At the gully's edge, lit up by Nancy's car headlights, was a plaque. Getting out of her car, Nancy walked over to the sign and read:

> At this spot Curtis Taylor, the greatest
> country-western entertainer in music
> history, met his tragic death. His fans
> will never forget him. He will live
> eternally in our hearts.

Nancy looked down the steep slope into the gully, then back at the road where her car waited, its flashers winking. A chill went through her.

How could a sober man possibly drive off that highway? Nancy wondered. It was fairly straight along the stretch. And why was the coroner's report so scanty? For five years those questions had been buried along with Curtis. Now Nancy was determined to find the answers. But the biggest question of all was, Who wanted Curtis Taylor dead?

Chapter

Four

"THANK GOODNESS you're back!" Louisa called from her dining room when Nancy walked in the front door. "We were worried about you."

Going back to the dining room, Nancy found George, Bess, and Louisa putting plates of pork chops, beans, and salad on the table.

"Where were you, Nan?" George asked. "One minute you were at the party, and the next you were gone."

"I checked out the coroner's report on Curtis," Nancy said, taking her place at the table. "Also, I took a ride up Route four-fifty-nine."

A dark cloud passed over Louisa's face when

she heard where Nancy had been, and she asked, "Where Curtis died? Did you learn anything?"

"Frankly, not much," Nancy answered with a weary sigh as she unfolded her napkin. "The report was really brief, but I wasn't able to talk to the coroner to find out why. How was the party?"

"Wild!" Bess answered, passing Nancy a large wooden salad bowl. "Tyrone gave us passes to Friday's dress rehearsal. Isn't that fantastic? And he asked me to be his personal assistant tomorrow."

George gave her cousin a teasing look, saying, "The emphasis of the job is definitely on the personal part."

Nancy grinned at Bess. "Great! What are you going to do for him?"

"Well, I'm going to keep track of his schedule. And if he wants a glass of water or something during a rehearsal, I'll get it. He said when I'm around he feels really good about himself. He even offered to pay me, but I said no. Can you believe it?

"Also, Tyrone sang today," Bess went on excitedly. "And he's even better in person than on tape."

"He sang 'Heartthrob,'" Louisa added, reaching for another pork chop, "and another one, called, 'Everything I Learned from You.' It's about Curtis, you can just tell."

"He was great," George agreed.

"Oh, and we talked to Malcolm Coleman and Billy Rutteridge," Bess said. "They both said they were at home with their wives the night Curtis died."

Nothing very interesting there, Nancy thought. She finished cutting herself a piece of bread, then looked at her friends, a serious expression in her blue eyes. "Well, I decided one thing today," she said. "I'm going to find out exactly what happened to Curtis Taylor five years ago."

Glancing at her cousin, George said, "But you're going to let us help you, aren't you?"

"Don't I always?" Nancy said with a grin.

"Come on, George," Nancy said the next morning after breakfast as she flipped through the pages of the Maywood phone book. "We've got a lawyer and a coroner to see."

"Have a great day, you two," Bess said, finishing her English muffin. "I know I will. Do I look okay?"

"Definitely," George said, glancing at the oversize pink sweater Bess was wearing over a short black skirt, with black and white striped tights and black ankle boots. Turning to Nancy, George asked, "Which lawyer are we going to see again?"

"Philip Hayward. The lawyer Curtis wrote that note to," Nancy answered. "When Louisa wakes up, tell her where we went, okay, Bess? Is she going with you to the Civic Center today?"

Bess shook her head. "She said something about getting her hair done and buying an outfit for Saturday's concert. She'll meet us back here tonight for dinner."

After saying goodbye, Nancy and George went out to Nancy's car and drove downtown. They parked in front of a building a dozen stories high, checked the directory in the lobby, then rode the elevator to Philip Hayward's law office on the tenth floor.

At first Hayward's secretary told the girls he wouldn't be able to see them. But when Nancy produced the note Curtis Taylor had written the night before his death, an empty space appeared in the lawyer's schedule. Soon Nancy and George were being ushered into an office with an Oriental rug and shiny brass lamps.

Mr. Hayward, a rotund man of about fifty, with silvery white hair and intense dark eyes, sat behind his wide desk, holding the note in his hands.

"Who are you, and where did you get this?" he asked gruffly, frowning at them over his reading glasses as he held Curtis's note.

Nancy introduced herself and George. Then they sat down and told him about how they'd found the tape and the letter.

"Nancy Drew, Nancy Drew," the attorney repeated, as if he might have heard her name before. "Are you any relation to—"

"Carson Drew? He's my father," Nancy replied.

Hayward smiled for the first time since the girls had entered his office. "How is Carson?" he exclaimed heartily. "I haven't seen him since the last Bar Association convention."

After telling him that her father was fine, Nancy said, "Mr. Hayward, we're concerned about this note, and about Curtis Taylor's death."

The lawyer's expression grew serious again. "I knew something was troubling Curtis before he died. We had an appointment for the morning after his death, in fact. I guess he was going to give me these things then." Shaking his head in amazement, he added, "I never would have guessed that someone was trying to kill him, though."

"Is there anyone you know of who might have wanted to do him harm?" Nancy added.

Hayward blew out his breath. "Well, I certainly don't want to accuse anyone of a crime he or she may not have committed." He gave Nancy and George a long look, then said, "This is strictly off the record, you understand. One person that comes to my mind is J. J. Rahmer."

Nancy tried to remember who J. J. Rahmer was. "Curtis's manager? Why him?"

"J.J. was Curtis's first manager," the lawyer explained. "Before I became Curtis's lawyer, he'd signed a terrible contract with J.J. A full forty percent of every dollar that Curtis earned went to Rahmer."

"Wow!" George interjected. "That's a lot."

"It's highway robbery, that's what it is," Hayward insisted. "I tried everything I could to get Curtis out of the contract, but it was ironclad. Curtis told me they had some pretty heavy fights about it, too."

"Wouldn't J.J. want his client alive and well, though?" Nancy asked, frowning.

The lawyer snorted, shaking his head in disgust. "I know this sounds crazy, but believe it or not, Curtis Taylor is worth as much to J.J. dead as he was alive. Even today, five years after his death, Curtis is a top-selling artist. And with Curtis gone, J.J. doesn't need his approval for any deals he might want to make, either."

Finally this case was going somewhere, Nancy thought. "Is there anyone else Curtis had problems with?" she asked.

Philip Hayward leaned back in his swivel chair and pressed the tips of his fingers together. "Well, I wouldn't say that Spike Wilson was very fond of Curtis, not at the end, anyway.

You see, Spike would miss rehearsals and show up late for recording sessions. Finally it got so bad that Curtis had to fire him and get another drummer. On the other hand, I'm fairly sure Spike was in the hospital the night Curtis died."

"What about Melanie Taylor?" Nancy asked. "Did she and Curtis have any problems that you know of?"

"Ah, the lovely Melanie," Hayward murmured. "A complex woman. Some people say she'd kill her own mother if it would help her career. Well, I know Curtis's fans were disappointed when he married her, because she comes off a little cold. But Curtis loved her— he told me so many times."

"But did she love him?" George wondered.

"That I can't rightly say," the lawyer answered. Glancing at his watch, he added, "I have a case to prepare, so if you'll excuse me now . . ."

Nancy and George quickly got to their feet. "You've been great, Mr. Hayward," Nancy said. "Thanks for talking to us."

"Let me offer you a little free advice," Hayward said, coming around his desk to walk the girls to the door. "As far as the law is concerned, Curtis Taylor's death was a certified accident. And maybe they're right. So don't go stepping on anybody's toes. Lawsuits are no fun at all."

"We'll keep that in mind," Nancy assured him. "Thanks again."

With that the girls left the office and headed back to Nancy's car.

"Well, Nan. You've definitely got a few suspects to check out," George said. "Where to now? Do you still want to talk to the coroner?"

Nancy nodded. "There's a map of Maywood in the glove compartment, George. Could you get it out and look up Overview Terrace? That's where Dexter Mobley lives, in a place called Windemere House."

When they got to Mobley's home, George shook her head in confusion. "I don't get it, Nancy," she said. "Coroners don't make that much money, do they? So how can this guy be spending his retirement years in a place for the ultrarich?"

Nancy looked up at the huge flagstone building on its beautifully landscaped grounds. "Maybe he comes from a rich family."

Parking in the visitors' lot, the two girls got out and headed for the building. Inside the reception area Nancy asked to see Dexter Mobley, telling the nurse that she was Mobley's grandniece. The girls followed the nurse down a hall.

"Here he is," the nurse announced cheerfully a few minutes later as she opened the door of a sun-filled room. "Your grandniece and her friend have come to see you, Mr. Mobley."

"Well, now," the old man said from his bed, eyeing the girls once the nurse had left. He was bald, with a sallow, unhealthy pallor and pale gray eyes. When he talked, Nancy could detect a slight wheeze.

"I didn't think I had a grandniece. Who, may I ask, are you?"

"Nancy Drew. If you don't mind, Mr. Mobley, we'd like to ask you a few questions about your report on Curtis Taylor's death."

Her statement could not have had a more dramatic effect. Mobley's face froze, losing what little color it had. "I have nothing to say about that," he growled. "Who sent you here?"

"Mr. Mobley," Nancy went on, ignoring the question, "we've discovered new information that leads us to believe Curtis Taylor may have been murdered. If we could know a little more about your report, we might—"

Nancy never got the chance to finish. The old man started shaking. With great effort he raised himself up on his elbows and glared at Nancy. "Are you accusing me of a cover-up? Well, you'll never be able to prove it!"

Nancy shot George a significant look. She hadn't even mentioned a cover-up. So why was

Dexter Mobley getting so worked up—unless there really *had* been one?

George let out a horrified gasp as the old man began shouting at the top of his lungs.

"Nurse! Nurse! Call the police. These girls are harassing me. They're trying to give me a heart attack!"

Chapter

Five

As Dexter Mobley raged, Nancy grabbed hold of a notepad near his bed and quickly jotted down Louisa's number.

"Nurse! Nurse!" Mobley screamed. "I said get them out of here!"

Trying to remain calm, Nancy put the pad back. "If you change your mind about talking," she told him, "I'm not with the police. I'm a private investigator, and my name is Nancy Drew. This is our number."

"Call the police!" he shouted.

"Come on, Nancy! Let's get out of here!" George cried, taking hold of her arm and pulling her toward the door.

The two girls fled for the exit, ignoring the calls of the nurse at the reception desk.

Once they were safely in Nancy's car and driving away from the nursing home, they couldn't help bursting out in relieved laughter.

"Nancy Drew," George said in a mock scolding tone, "you get me in more trouble."

"That was pretty intense," Nancy said.

"I'll say," George added. Growing more serious, she said, "I can't believe he went bananas like that. Why did he say that about a cover-up? Do you think there could have been a payoff? Maybe that's how he's able to live in such a posh place."

Nancy nodded. "I was thinking the same thing, George."

After a quick lunch in a fast-food place, Nancy and George drove to the Civic Center to tell Bess and Tyrone what they had found out.

They parked in the crowded lot, and Nancy led the way to the huge, arched entrance. After pulling open a wide glass door, the two girls stepped into the Civic Center lobby. The center had a wall of glass that shot up at least three stories, with escalators going to top levels. From the upper tier gigantic crystal chandeliers were suspended in the air. "This place is beautiful," Nancy said.

"Oh, no," George said, eyeing the crowds. Security guards were turning everyone away at the entrance to the auditorium. "I hope they'll let us in."

"Sorry, folks," Nancy heard one guard say. "You'll have to wait for tomorrow to see the show."

The girls went over to the auditorium door, where they were stopped by a security guard wearing a light gray uniform. "May I help you?" he asked.

"We're meeting a friend inside," Nancy said.

A dubious look crossed the man's face. "You and everybody else," he said with a sigh. "Sorry, girls. We're closed to the public today. There's a technical rehearsal going on in there."

Nancy was about to explain further when George called, "Eddie!" Turning, Nancy saw the tall, blond guy George had been dancing with at the press party walking through the lobby toward them.

Eddie's face lit up the minute he saw George. "Hi! Are you here to see me?" he asked, looking flattered. "They're okay, Jim," he said to the guard, who stepped aside so they could pass.

The girls exchanged a pleased look as they followed Eddie down the red-carpeted aisle toward the stage. Onstage a crew of about a dozen were setting up a series of huge mirrored balls, with multicolored mirrored backdrops.

"Wow, what a concert this is going to be," Nancy said, looking around.

With a smile Eddie said, "Pretty nice, huh? So what can I do for you two?"

"Actually, we're looking for our friend Bess," George told him. "Do you remember her from the party? She's short, with straight blond hair?"

"You mean Tyrone's good luck charm?" Eddie said with a laugh. "Sure. Everybody knows Bess."

Nancy and George grinned at each other. Obviously Bess had made a big impression her first day on the job.

"She and Tyrone just stepped out for some lunch, though," Eddie continued. "They should be back in a little while. Why don't you wait out here in the audience? Melanie's going to be rehearsing one of her tunes."

"But I thought this was a technical rehearsal," Nancy said. "Doesn't that mean it's just for adjusting the lights and stuff like that?"

"That's usually true," Eddie explained, "but Melanie's a little nervous about performing for a large crowd. She wants the extra rehearsal."

Onstage the lighting technicians were folding up their ladders as another crew ambled on to set up instruments.

From an unseen microphone Nancy and George heard a firm female voice boom

48

through the concert hall: "I'm going to run a test on those lights while Melanie's people set up."

"Who's that?" George asked, looking around for the disembodied voice.

Eddie took George by the shoulders and spun her around so she was facing the back of the concert hall. "See that little window up there?" he said, pointing to it. "My boss, Marjorie Cooper, is up there. She's the director of the gala."

Looking toward the stage, Nancy saw the lights begin to change from a yellowish-white glow to a rosy color, then to deep purple.

"Beautiful effect," said Marjorie Cooper. "Nice work, guys. Since Melanie isn't here yet, could we have a look at Tyrone's neon guitar? Is Eddie there?"

With a quick wink for George, Eddie rushed up the aisle and onto the stage. "Here I am, Marge," he said, waving toward the little window he'd shown George.

"Eddie, would you stand in for Tyrone while we run a lighting test on that neon instrument?" Marjorie asked.

"We might as well have a seat until Bess and Tyrone get back," Nancy said as Eddie disappeared backstage. She walked up the aisle and plopped down in a plush deep red velvet seat.

Soon Eddie appeared onstage holding a multicolored guitar, and the director's amplified voice said, "Okay, let's see what it looks like."

Suddenly the stage and the hall were plunged into darkness. "What's going on?" George murmured. An instant later there was a burst of color onstage, all coming from the neon guitar and reflected in the onstage mirrors. "That's intense," George said.

"Nice effect," the director said as the lights came up. "Thank you, Eddie."

Just then Melanie appeared from the side of the stage, followed by several musicians. She was shading her eyes from the brilliant lights above her. "Marge?" she called, peering up at the back of the immense hall. "Are you ready for me?"

"Sure, Melanie," the director answered.

Melanie stepped over to where her band had assembled and shared a few words with the keyboard player. Then she walked forward on the stage.

"You're on right after the Blue Mountain Boys finish," Marjorie said.

"We'll start with 'Losing My Heart,'" Melanie said.

"Right," the director said.

Leaning toward Nancy, George whispered, "Melanie looks so small on that big stage, doesn't she?"

Nancy's answer was cut off by Melanie's band, which began a loud, driving beat that dropped quickly to an urgent hush. Melanie stood center stage, her arms at her sides.

"I didn't mean to lose my heart," she began, half singing and half speaking in a quiet whisper. "It just happened that way. . . ." Then her voice swelled to a note that sent goose bumps all up and down Nancy's arms. "But now I'm lost in the feeling, and it won't go away!"

"Wow," Nancy murmured.

Melanie's voice seemed to sweep over the hall like liquid velvet. "Oh, darlin', oh, darlin', let's make this moment stay . . . 'cause I'm losing my heart to you—ooo!"

For the rest of the song Nancy, George, and everyone else in the hall were absolutely transfixed by the beautiful singer. When Melanie was done, no one applauded. If the others were affected the way I was, Nancy thought, they're too paralyzed to clap.

"Was that okay, Marge?" Melanie asked when she was finished.

From the booth came a little chuckle. "Not half bad. You'll do," the director said.

Instead of exiting backstage, Melanie waved to someone behind where Nancy and George were sitting. Turning around, Nancy noticed a tall, heavyset man with blow-dried blond hair about twenty rows back. He waved to Melanie, and the singer hurried offstage and down the aisle, not noticing Nancy or George. When Nancy turned around again, she saw Melanie falling into the man's arms. They were sharing a passionate kiss.

George lifted an eyebrow and shot Nancy a look. "Check that out," she murmured. "I wonder who he is?"

"Nancy! George!" came Bess's bubbling voice from the stage. "Hi."

The two girls turned to see Bess and Tyrone waving to them from the stairs leading up to the stage. "Want to come back to Greenwood?" he called out.

"Don't you have work to do here?" Nancy inquired, getting up and walking toward the huge stage with George.

"My assistant here has arranged for a stand-in to handle it," Tyrone replied, grinning down at Bess and putting an arm around her. "It's just a matter of adjusting the lights. Besides . . ." Tyrone's voice dropped as Nancy and George came closer. "I want to check out that other song, remember? The one we found in my uncle's closet?"

Bess's blue eyes were shining as she asked Nancy, "Did you guys find anything out from the coroner or that lawyer?"

After Nancy and George explained what they had found out that day, Tyrone let out a low whistle. "You mean to say it could have been Melanie, J. J. Rahmer, *or* Spike Wilson who murdered Uncle Curtis? They also happen to be the three people who are at Greenwood all the time. I'm surrounded by potential murderers."

"J.J.'s staying there, too?" George inquired.

Tyrone nodded. "He's from Nashville, but he's going to be staying at the house while Melanie records an album at the studio there, once this gala's over."

Nancy looked quickly around the auditorium. "I don't see Melanie anywhere now. If she's gone back to Greenwood, maybe I can ask all three of our suspects some questions while we're there."

"Let's get a move on, then," Tyrone said.

When the group arrived at Greenwood, Vickers hurried out of the mansion to greet them. "Did you forget your photo session, sir?" the butler asked hurriedly. "The photographer's been here quite some time. He's waiting in the formal living room. I tried to reach you—"

Bess gasped, saying, "You never mentioned any photo session, Tyrone."

"I guess I forgot," he said sheepishly. "Well, it shouldn't take long, anyway. They're just going to take a few shots for a magazine article. You girls can come with me, if you like."

"Sure," Bess said. "Come on, guys."

Just then Nancy caught sight of Spike Wilson in jeans and a heavy sweater, reading a newspaper in the small gazebo near the mansion.

"You go ahead," she told her friends as Tyrone strode toward the mansion's front entrance. "I want to talk to Spike."

"You're sure you don't want us to come with you?" George asked. When Nancy shook her head, George and Bess followed Tyrone inside.

Nancy sauntered over to the gazebo, taking a few breaths of the crisp fall air. "This is really lovely," she commented lightly, gesturing toward the deep red asters planted around the gazebo.

"Are you talking to me?" Spike said gruffly, looking up from his copy of the *Scoop.* Nancy's quick eyes went to the page he'd been reading. "Curtis will be there!" the headlines screamed. "Psychics predict star's return at anniversary gala."

"Aren't you Spike Wilson, the drummer?" Nancy asked with a smile. When he nodded, she added, "I saw you in the studio suite yesterday, but I wasn't sure if it was really you."

"Oh, it was me all right," Spike said, sounding a little bored. "I kind of do a little of everything around here." Then he turned back to his paper.

Looking at the ex-drummer, Nancy tried to think of a way to get him to open up to her. "I think your solo on 'Loose as a Goose' was really great," she finally said, trying to sound very impressed. "Do you give autographs?"

Spike snorted bitterly. "Oh, I gave plenty in my time."

"Then please give me one," Nancy said, smiling brightly. "It would be a real honor." She reached in her handbag and quickly pulled out a piece of paper and a pen.

Looking embarrassed, Spike scrawled his name and handed it back to her.

"Will you be playing at the concert, too?" Nancy asked, trying to sound hopeful.

"No," Spike told her. "I don't play anymore. My wrist was injured a few years back." As he spoke, Spike's eyes turned toward a sleek gray limo that was pulling up to the mansion. When it stopped, Melanie and the tall, heavyset man she'd kissed at the Civic Center got out.

"Who's that?" Nancy asked.

She noticed that Spike's brown eyes softened as he told her, "That's Melanie Taylor."

"I mean the man," Nancy pressed.

"Oh, him. J. J. Rahmer," Spike answered. His eyes followed J.J. and Melanie as they made their way to the mansion, and Nancy noticed the muscles in his jaw tightening.

Perfect! Nancy thought. Her three main suspects were all in the same place. And two of them had a romance going. Spike didn't seem very happy about seeing J.J., she noticed. Nancy wasn't sure what it all meant, or if it even had anything to do with Curtis's death, but she was determined to find out.

Turning back to Spike, Nancy asked, "Is J.J. a musician, too?"

"Are you kidding?" Spike answered contemptuously. "The only talent he has is for taking advantage of people. He's what you call a manager."

"You don't think much of him, do you?" Nancy observed.

Spike cast a sharp look her way but didn't answer.

"Melanie seems awfully fond of him," Nancy pressed.

Closing his paper in disgust, Spike said, "Yeah, well, snakes have their charms, I guess. Excuse me." With that he strode toward the mansion.

As Nancy watched him go, she realized that she hadn't even been able to ask Spike about Curtis Taylor's death. After going to the front door, she rang the bell, and Vickers led her to the studio, where the others were waiting.

"The photo shoot's over so soon?" she asked Tyrone.

He looked up from where he was showing Bess the sound studio's audio controls and smiled. "I told you it'd be fast."

Then, walking over to Nancy, Tyrone fished a set of keys and a business card from his jeans pockets and handed them to her. "I want you to have these. This key will get you into the mansion, and this one's for the studio closet," he said, his voice filled with somber determination. "I've been thinking. With this concert and all, I'm going to be pretty busy. I told Vickers and the other security guys that you're to have the run of the house. The telephone number here is on that card. I want to make sure nothing gets in the way of your finding the scoundrel."

"Thanks," Nancy said. "I'm hoping we'll have enough evidence to convince the police to reopen this case soon."

Going back into the sound studio, Tyrone flipped on the switch of the electronic keyboard and pressed the cassette deck to the record position. Then he took the music for "Melanie" from his pocket. "Maybe this song will help us," he said.

Just as he was about to start playing the song, Nancy heard a thumping noise outside the door, followed by the sound of receding footsteps.

Tyrone straightened up, looking at Nancy in alarm. "Did you hear what I heard?" he whispered.

"I sure did," Nancy said, striding toward the door. "Somebody's been spying on us!"

Chapter

Six

NANCY HURRIED to the door of the studio suite and yanked it open with a swift tug, then stepped into the hallway. It was empty.

"Bess, George, go left!" she called back to her friends. Turning right, Nancy followed the corridor to where it turned again. Still no one. She raced to the end of the hall and turned right again. Suddenly she bumped smack into someone coming the other way—J. J. Rahmer.

"Whoa, miss!" the heavyset man said, grabbing hold of her elbow to help her recover her balance. "Where are you running to so fast?"

Nancy scrutinized him carefully, but the cool smile on Rahmer's face gave away nothing. If he had scuttled off, then turned around and come back toward the studio suite, he was sure covering up well. "I'm, uh, just looking for someone," Nancy hedged.

"Oh? Who's that? Maybe I can help you."

Just then Bess and George rounded the corridor. "Nancy!" Bess cried.

"There you are," Nancy said, pretending Bess and George were the ones she'd been looking for all along. Flashing Rahmer a smile, she took her friends by the arm and walked back toward the studio.

"Did you two see anyone?" Nancy whispered when they were a safe distance from J. J. Rahmer.

"We heard someone running, but we didn't see who it was," George answered.

"Well, whoever was listening definitely heard us talking about the case," Nancy said.

"We'd better watch our backs," Bess said, shivering.

In the studio suite Tyrone looked worried when the girls relayed the warning to him. But all he said was, "Well, let's record this tune, anyhow."

"Good idea," Nancy agreed with a smile.

After locking the suite's outer door, the girls joined Tyrone in the soundproof recording room. First Tyrone picked out the melody of the song on the keyboard. Then he hit a button on the audio panel, and the recorder started rolling. " 'Melanie,' take one," he said into the microphone, then picked up his acoustic guitar.

"Oh, Melanie, Melanie, Melanie," Tyrone crooned, reading from the music as he strummed the guitar. "You are the only one for me. . . ."

Nancy didn't know what she had expected. Having heard other Curtis Taylor songs, she thought "Melanie" would have a richer melody line and more interesting lyrics.

"You left me, and now you're with him.
Someday he'll be gone, though,
And your heart I'll win. . . . "

Nancy shook her head in dismay. Maybe Curtis had written the song in a hurry, or maybe it was just an unsuccessful attempt. "You left me, and now you're with him. . . ." Who did Curtis mean?

When the music died down into silence and Tyrone shut off the tape recorder, Nancy cleared her throat. "Well," she said. "That was . . . enlightening."

"Bad, you mean," Tyrone said matter-of-factly. "Worst song Uncle Curtis ever wrote, if you ask me. Still," he added as he set up the machine to make a cassette copy for Nancy, "maybe there's a clue in it for us."

There had to be one, Nancy thought. But after listening to the song she still had no idea what it was. Melanie, J.J., Spike—they were all suspects. But which one was implicated in the song? Or was it someone they hadn't even considered?

"Did Melanie ever leave Curtis?" Nancy asked Tyrone as she paced back and forth in front of the tape deck. "Did they ever have any sort of separation?"

Tyrone shook his head. "Not that I know of. And I think I would know about it if they had."

"Maybe the song isn't supposed to be auto-biographical," Bess pointed out.

"Then why call it 'Melanie'?" George asked.

"And why did Uncle Curtis want me to hear it?" Tyrone added, looking stumped.

When the cassette copy was made, Nancy took it from Tyrone. "I want to study this song," she said. "Maybe Louisa will be able to help. After all, she's a Curtis Taylor expert. Could I have the music sheet, too? You never know."

"Here you go," Tyrone replied, handing it to her. "And good luck."

"Hi, girls," Louisa called from the kitchen when Nancy, Bess, and George arrived back at her house.

Walking into the kitchen, they discovered Louisa tossing a salad. A pan of steaming lasagna was resting on the stove.

"You look great, Aunt Louisa," George said, picking out a piece of lettuce and munching on it.

Looking pleased, Louisa patted her hair, which had been curled and highlighted. "I bought a great dress, too," she said. "Wait until you girls see it. How was your day?"

The girls got to work setting the kitchen table while they told Louisa all that had happened.

"I bet it was Melanie," Louisa insisted as they all sat down at the table and served themselves.

"We don't have proof of that yet, Aunt Louisa," Nancy cautioned. "There is something you could do to help me out, though. Would you go over this song of Curtis's with me? There's got to be a clue in it somewhere, and you know his music so well."

"Of course," Louisa agreed at once. "I'll be glad to help in any way I can. But I'll tell you what I think right now. The clue's in the title. Curtis knew Melanie wanted to kill him so she could inherit his money."

Nancy stared hard at Louisa. "I know you don't like Melanie, but why would she have wanted to kill Curtis? She already had his name and all the money she wanted. She even had his help in establishing her own career."

"Hah!" Louisa snorted. "You don't know her, Nancy. I read in the *Scoop* that she was a madwoman about having to share the estate with Tyrone. And you saw how she was with us."

"Well, maybe we should try to figure out the lyrics," George said. "How does it start again? 'You left me, and now you're with him. . . .'"

Nancy nodded. "What do you make of that, Louisa?"

Shaking her head, Louisa insisted, "It's the title that tells everything. That was Curtis's way of naming his future murderer."

Just as the girls were finishing the dishes the phone rang. "Want me to get it?" Bess asked. When Louisa nodded, Bess went over to the wall phone and picked up the receiver. "It's for you, Nancy," she said a moment later.

It's probably Dad, Nancy thought, calling to find out how I am. But she was wrong.

"Nancy Drew?" came a tense masculine voice that sounded as if it belonged to an older person.

"Yes," Nancy said expectantly. "This is Nancy."

"Dexter Mobley here," the voice said.

The former coroner! Nancy thought, growing excited. He was calling her after all.

"I, er, reconsidered about calling you. Luckily, the paper with your number was still on the floor here. I, er . . . I would like to speak with you about Curtis Taylor, if you're still interested."

"Yes, I am," Nancy said, trying to stay calm. "Go ahead."

"No, no, not . . . over the . . . phone," the feeble man insisted, coughing between words. "Come out to the home. It's after visiting hours, but I'm sure I can get the staff to let you in."

"I'll be there right away." Nancy hung up and looked at the clock on the wall. It was nine o'clock. "Dexter Mobley wants me to go talk to him about Curtis's death!" she exclaimed. "Anybody want to go with me?"

"You mean the coroner?" George asked, her brown eyes widening in surprise. "Let's go!" She put away a plate and reached for her handbag.

"I'm coming, too," Bess put in.

"Here's a house key," Louisa said, reaching for a key from a hook by the back door. "See you in the morning, I guess."

Nancy took the key. Then she, Bess, and George grabbed their coats and ran out the door.

"I have a feeling this is going to be big," Nancy told her friends as they piled into the car.

Windemere House was quiet and dark when the girls got there fifteen minutes later. They hurried up to the desk in the dimly lit reception area. "Hello," Nancy told a young man who was behind the counter. "We're here to see Mr. Dexter Mobley. It's urgent."

"Visiting hours are over," the nurse said dryly.

Nancy smiled patiently. "Yes, I know that, but he called me especially. He needs to see me *now*."

The man gave her a long look before saying, "I'll check." Then he dialed a number on the phone in front of him. "Sorry to disturb you, Mr. Mobley," he said into the receiver, "but—" Apparently, Dexter Mobley interrupted the receptionist. After a moment the young man turned to Nancy and asked, "Are you Nancy Drew?"

"Yes," Nancy told him.

"You can go in," he told Nancy. "But you'll have to go alone. And please don't stay longer than five minutes. I'm really not supposed to let anyone in at this hour, even if a resident requests a visitor."

"We'll wait for you here," George said. "And good luck, Nan."

With a wave Nancy went down the hall and knocked on Mobley's door. "Come in," said a shaky voice. Nancy pushed the door open and went inside.

Maybe it was the dim light, Nancy thought, but Dexter Mobley looked a lot worse than he had earlier. His hands were shaking visibly, and his face was pale and haggard. "I've been thinking about what you said," he told Nancy in a weak voice. "What makes you think Curtis Taylor was murdered?"

When Nancy told him about the cassette and music Tyrone had found in Curtis's costume, the old man sank back into his pillows. His eyes darted back and forth across the ceiling, and his breathing grew more labored.

"Take it easy, okay?" Nancy told him, putting a hand on his arm. It was ice cold.

"There's something I never told anybody. But now that I'm . . . so sick . . ." His chest heaved, and tears formed in his eyes. "It's a terrible burden. I want to be rid of it."

Nancy nodded. This definitely sounded big.

The old coroner's lip trembled. "I changed . . . changed my report," he said softly.

Nancy stood very still, holding her breath.

"I never thought—*nobody* thought Curtis could have been murdered." Dexter Mobley tried to raise himself on his elbows. Nancy helped him, putting a pillow behind his head. "You see, there were barbiturates in his blood. A very high level. But I naturally assumed he'd taken them knowingly."

"You mean, you thought he killed *himself* with barbiturates?" Nancy asked, stunned.

"Y-yes. But I never mentioned them in my report. *He* persuaded me not to, said it would ruin Curtis's reputa—" The old man broke off in a fit of coughing.

Nancy's heart was racing. "You didn't want to ruin Curtis's reputation," she finished for him. "Somebody persuaded you to leave the barbiturates out of your report. Who?"

"He told me Curtis's fans—Curtis was their hero, and if they knew he was a drug addict . . ." Mobley struggled to sit up straight. His face was darkening. "But you've got to believe me. I never thought it could be murder! I'll give back the money. All of it. I'll be gone soon, anyway." He grabbed her arm. "I swear I didn't think it was murder. Please believe me," he pleaded.

As she tried to get the former coroner to lie back down, Nancy said, "I believe you, Mr. Mobley." A glance at the clock told her her five minutes were just about up. "I need to know one other thing," she said quickly. "I need to know *who* persuaded you to change your report. Who was it, sir?"

Just then the door opened, and the nurse came in, gesturing for her to leave.

"I have to know, Mr. Mobley. It's very important," Nancy said urgently.

"Sorry, Ms. Drew," said the nurse. "You'll have to go now. You can see that whatever this is about, it's upsetting the patient."

The next thing Nancy knew, the young man was guiding her forcefully toward the door.

As Nancy was being herded out of the room, she heard Dexter Mobley say the name:

"Rahmer. J. J. Rahmer."

Chapter

Seven

J. J. RAHMER! For a brief second Nancy locked eyes with the former coroner. "Thank you so much," she said gratefully.

As the nurse stepped behind her to force her from the room, Nancy saw the old man nod, and she thought she detected a hint of relief in his eyes.

After leaving the room, she hurried down the corridor to where George and Bess were waiting.

"Any luck?" Bess asked Nancy anxiously.

Without slowing down, Nancy gestured to her friends to follow her out the door. Once outside she told them about the barbiturates found in Curtis Taylor's blood and about Rahmer's role in the cover-up.

"Very interesting," George murmured from the passenger seat as Nancy drove back toward Louisa's.

Shaking her head, Bess added thoughtfully, "Suicide, huh? But that doesn't make sense. I still can remember those antidrug ads Curtis Taylor made. They were great. I really hate to think he didn't practice what he preached."

Shooting Bess a significant look, Nancy cautioned, "We shouldn't jump to any conclusions. Just because there were barbiturates in his blood doesn't mean that Curtis put them there. A killer could have found a way to slip them to him, maybe in the drink Curtis had before he left the house that night."

"Of course," George murmured. "I didn't think of that."

"Don't feel bad," Nancy said. "Neither did the coroner. Neither did anyone else, till Tyrone found that packet."

When they pulled into Louisa's driveway, the girls saw that the house was dark, except for the yellow glare of the front porch light. Once inside they tiptoed over to the small stairway that led to the upper level.

"Good night, Nan. I guess we have a lot to sleep on tonight," George whispered, her hand on the doorknob of the room she and Bess were staying in.

Nancy opened the door of her room, taking

care to be quiet. "I'll say," she whispered before she went inside. "Good night, you guys. Get a good rest, because tomorrow's going to be a very big day."

"See you in the morning," Bess added.

"Well, I can tell you one thing, absolutely for sure—Curtis Taylor never in his life abused drugs, never!" Louisa insisted the next morning at breakfast after Nancy, Bess, and George had filled Louisa in on their visit to the former coroner.

"How can you know that, Aunt Louisa?" Bess asked. "He was under a lot of pressure, being a star and all."

Louisa put down her fork and shook her head in disgust. "Curtis was a clean-living man. Anybody who listens to his music knows that. Living right was his whole message."

Nancy's gut feeling was to agree with Louisa, but she still needed proof. "Well, maybe J. J. Rahmer will be able to enlighten us about what happened five years ago. Tyrone said he was staying at Greenwood, right? But I'm not sure if I should try to find him there or at the Civic Center."

Bess looked up suddenly and said, "Oh—I forgot to tell you guys. The Blue Mountain Boys are hosting a pre-gala party at their hotel today, complete with bluegrass music and tons of food. We're all invited, thanks to Tyrone. He said he'd come pick us up. What do you guys say—do you want to go?"

"What a great way to pass the time before tonight's dress rehearsal," said Louisa, getting up to boil water for another cup of tea.

"Tyrone said the same thing," Bess said. "The day before a concert most singers like to relax and give their 'pipes' a rest. Anyway," she added, turning to Nancy, "if J.J.'s not at Greenwood, I'll bet he'll be at the party. You can join us there."

"Good idea," George put in. "I'll go with you to Greenwood if you want, Nan."

With a sheepish smile Louisa said, "If you don't mind, Nancy, I'd like to go to this party with Bess. It sounds too good to pass up."

"No problem," Nancy told her, laughing. "But do me a favor, okay, Bess? Tell Tyrone what the coroner said about J.J. He should know about it."

Bess nodded. She got up from the table and hurried out of the room, then returned a moment later with two tickets. "Here are the passes to the party. It's at the Imperial Hotel, right next to the Civic Center."

Taking the passes from Bess, Nancy said, "Thanks, Bess. I just hope we can find J.J. and get to the bottom of this mystery soon."

"This is unbelievable," George murmured as Nancy inched her car through the heavy traffic on her way to Greenwood. Passing the entrance to the visitors' parking lot, Nancy glimpsed a sign that read Full. A uniformed worker was pointing to the sign and waving cars past. Still, a lot of cars crawled as slowly as they could in front of the grounds. Nancy guessed they were trying to get a peek at the estate through the bushes lining the property.

Finally Nancy managed to get to the estate's private security gate. There, she gave her name, and the guard motioned her through. After parking, Nancy and George walked up to the mansion and rang the bell.

"Good morning, Ms. Drew," Vickers said when he opened the door a moment later. "I'm afraid Mr. Taylor has already left for the Imperial Hotel. Is there anything I can help you with?"

"As a matter of fact, it's J. J. Rahmer we've come to see. Is he here?" Nancy asked.

The butler nodded. "I'll inform Mr. Rahmer that you're here, ladies," he said, bowing his head. "Although I must warn you, he is not in the best of spirits this morning. He and Mrs. Taylor seem to be experiencing some, er, personal conflicts."

Nancy frowned, trying to think of a way to make sure the manager would speak with her and George. Suddenly an idea struck her.

"If you wouldn't mind, Vickers, maybe you can tell Mr. Rahmer that in addition to being friends of Tyrone's, my friend and I are journalists from, uh, *Melody Monthly,*" she said, citing the name of a popular music magazine.

For a moment George looked at Nancy as if she'd lost her mind. Then George recovered her composure, adding, "Yes, we're sure our readers will be interested in learning about Melanie Taylor's accomplished manager. But if we don't get our story in today, he'll miss being featured in next month's edition."

Vickers raised an eyebrow. "Indeed," he said calmly, but Nancy thought she detected a hint of a smile on his lips. "I'll inform Mr. Rahmer right away."

The butler disappeared down the hall. A few minutes later, J. J. Rahmer strode into the entry hall to greet them, a pleasant smile on his face.

"I wish I had known about this earlier," he said. "But I'll be happy to accommodate you however I can. Shall we go upstairs to my suite? It's quieter there."

Following Rahmer up the wide marble staircase, Nancy crossed her fingers. She hoped she and George could pull off the interview.

"Now, how can I help you?" Rahmer asked, motioning for them to sit down at a small mahogany table in the outer room of his guest suite.

Starting amiably, Nancy and George asked Rahmer how he had first met Curtis Taylor, and what Rahmer's strategy had been in those early days. Nancy wrote down what he told her in a small notepad she always carried in her purse. She couldn't help being amazed at the easy way J.J. seemed to take credit for everything Curtis Taylor had ever accomplished.

When the manager seemed relaxed and comfortable, Nancy decided to make her move. "Mr. Rahmer, we all know that Curtis Taylor was a notable antidrug spokesperson. But what can you tell us about the persistent rumors that he actually abused barbiturates?"

If he was disturbed by what she had said, J. J. Rahmer didn't let on. "I never heard any such rumors," he said, dismissing them with a chuckle. "I suppose all famous people are subject to manufactured misinformation about them, however. I guess it's just the price of fame."

"But these rumors are so specific, sir," Nancy persisted. "It's even said that his fatal accident may have been caused by them. Some people seem to think that the coroner was actually paid to participate in a cover-up because there were drugs discovered in Mr. Taylor's blood."

At that Rahmer took a sharp intake of breath and glanced at his watch. "Ladies, I hate to end this interview suddenly, but I've just realized that I'm late for my next appointment. I'm sorry, but I must ask you to leave right away." The manager stood and indicated the door.

"Are you saying you don't know anything about barbiturates in Mr. Taylor's blood?" George tried one more time.

"Why, that's utter nonsense," Rahmer said with a stiff smile, walking the girls toward the door. "Not worthy of a reply."

"And what about the notion that Curtis Taylor was murdered?" Nancy blurted out.

At that, J.J. stopped in his tracks, his face flushed. "Murdered?" he repeated shakily before the unflappable expression came back over his features. "That, too, is just so much nonsense! You ladies are beginning to sound like you're from the *Weekly Scoop*," he added angrily. "I certainly hope I haven't been duped into giving that rag an interview. Because if I have, I shall certainly ask my lawyer to sue. Good day!"

Rahmer opened the door and glared at Nancy and George until they left the suite. Then he unceremoniously slammed the door behind them.

Out in the hall Nancy and George walked far enough away from his door so that they wouldn't be heard. "He was stonewalling," Nancy whispered. "And he did a pretty good job of it, too."

"If I didn't know better, I would have believed him when he said he didn't know anything about Curtis and the barbiturates," George said. "What a terrific liar."

Just then they heard Rahmer's suite door open.

"George, in here," Nancy whispered, tugging on her friend's arm. Quickly the two girls stepped through open double French doors into what looked like a library. Flattening themselves against the inside wall next to the doorway, they waited until they heard Rahmer stride quickly and purposefully past them and down the corridor. Nancy heard him stop and open a door not too far away.

"I wish you would knock before you come in here," came Melanie's voice, and then the door shut, muffling her next words.

Taking a careful step forward, with George close behind her, Nancy leaned forward and peered into the empty hallway. "Come on," she mouthed to George.

The two girls tiptoed down the corridor, moving closer to the door through which Rahmer and Melanie's voices could be heard.

"And I don't need any more stress, today of all days," Melanie said, sounding angry. "You've already upset me enough by asking me to agree to such terrible terms on my next album."

"Well, darling, that's nothing compared to

the problems you have now," Rahmer told her.

"What kinds of problems?" came Melanie's frustrated voice.

"I'm referring to the small matter of your late husband's death," Rahmer told her. Nancy and George exchanged a startled look.

"Those reporter friends of Tyrone's told me that there are rumors going around that Curtis was murdered," Rahmer continued. "Did you know that?"

"Murdered? That's a new one," Melanie scoffed. "But so what? I've lived with stupid rumors for years. Besides, these at least don't have anything to do with me."

Nancy's breath caught in her throat as she listened to Rahmer's reply.

"Come now, darling," he told her. "How do you intend to explain away the three-million-dollar insurance policy you took out on your dear deceased husband?"

There was a beat of silence before Melanie replied to his question. "I had every right to get that policy, and you know it!" she protested at last. "Wives take out insurance on their husbands' lives all the time."

"Oh?" Rahmer challenged. "But do those other wives buy that insurance the very day before their husbands are found dead? Like you did?"

Chapter
Eight

NANCY RAISED HER EYEBROWS and looked at George as they took in this new information. Three million dollars in insurance money would be considered a motive for murder in any court.

"Get out of here, you creep!" Melanie cried out. "You're accusing me of these crazy things because you're jealous. You know there will always be another man between us. I must have been insane to think you had anything to offer me. No wonder Curtis hated you."

Those angry words were followed by the sound of a crash. "Whoa," Rahmer said bitterly. "The truth really hurts."

Nancy and George wondered what Melanie had thrown at Rahmer.

"What would you know about the truth?" Melanie shrieked. "You get out of here." Another crash came, then she yelled, "Get out this instant!"

Moving like lightning, Nancy pulled George away from the door, and the two raced back to the library doorway. There they waited until they heard Rahmer leave Melanie's room and tramp down the marble stairway.

"Whew," George said, blowing out a big breath. "Three million dollars!"

Nancy nodded. "And Melanie was the only person who was with Curtis the night he died, according to all the newspapers."

An excited gleam came into George's eyes, and she whispered, "Then maybe she's the one who put the barbiturates in his drink."

"But it was J.J. who bribed the coroner, George," Nancy pointed out. "I suppose he could have done it to protect Melanie, though."

"Good thinking, Nan. Maybe he was in love with her, even back then."

That certainly seemed possible, Nancy thought. "George, remember, Curtis got a phone call that night. That's supposedly why he left the house."

"Supposedly?" George echoed, arching an eyebrow.

"Wasn't it Melanie who said someone phoned for Curtis before he left the house? Maybe she was lying," Nancy suggested.

"I don't know," George said thoughtfully. "But I know who might. Come on. Let's go find Vickers."

The girls walked quietly down the corridor to the stairway near the mansion entrance. A uniformed maid was cleaning the squares of glass in the upper part of the door.

"Excuse me," Nancy asked her. "Do you know where we can find Vickers?"

"I think he's in the kitchen," the maid answered. She pointed down the corridor. "It's to the left, at the end of the hall."

Following the maid's directions, the girls found themselves in a huge kitchen filled with industrial appliances. Vickers sat inspecting silver at a table in a glassed-in alcove facing a garden.

"Vickers," Nancy called from the doorway. "May we have a word with you?"

"Of course," he replied, looking up from the silverware. "How can I help you?"

Nancy and George stepped over to the alcove, and Nancy asked, "Were you on duty the night Curtis Taylor died?"

The butler's face took on a sad expression. "I'm afraid not," he replied, shaking his head. "Mr. Taylor died on a Wednesday evening, which was the staff's customary day off at that time."

"Then you wouldn't know if he really received a phone call that night," George said with a hint of defeat in her voice.

"No, I wouldn't. Sorry."

"Oh, well," Nancy said. "Thanks anyway."

"Why are you talking about the night my husband died?" a woman's voice spoke out suddenly from behind the girls. "Curtis has been gone for five years now. Isn't it time to let it rest?"

Whipping her head around, Nancy saw Melanie Taylor standing in the doorway. She was wearing a long robe, and her face was stained with tears.

"Mrs. Taylor!" Nancy said in surprise.

"Melanie, if you please," the singer said, walking up to Nancy and George. She walked over to the girls, looking them up and down, a thoughtful expression on her pretty face. Nancy noticed that Vickers rose silently from the table and slipped away.

"All right, I'll ask," Melanie said finally. "Who are you?"

"We're friends of Tyrone's," George answered.

"Yes, I know all that," Melanie said, dismissing what George had said. "But who are you *really?* And why are you in my house?"

Nancy decided to be honest, hoping it would

shock Melanie into revealing useful information. "Tyrone has asked us to look into your husband's death, Melanie," Nancy said. "We have reason to believe his 'accident' was actually murder."

There was a long moment of silence. "Is that so?" the singer asked, more weary than shocked. She pulled out a stool and sat down next to George. "What sort of reasons?" she challenged.

As Nancy told her about the packet Tyrone had found in his uncle's jacket, Melanie's face remained impassive. Her gray eyes flickered when Nancy mentioned the presence of drugs in his blood, but still, her basic demeanor was cool.

When Nancy was finished, Melanie nodded slowly. "You know, for five years I've resisted thinking about that night," she said softly, a sad expression on her face. "But somewhere deep down inside me, I've always felt something was . . . *wrong* about it. Maybe Curtis really was murdered."

Only when she said the word *murdered* did Nancy notice a tiny tear falling from one of Melanie's eyes. Suddenly the singer let out a heart-wrenching sob. Her head fell to the counter, and she moaned, "Oh, Curtis, Curtis, if only I'd even suspected. I would have never let you go that night."

If this was an act, it was one of the best

Nancy had ever seen. But then, she reminded herself, Melanie's performing abilities had been artfully proven to her just yesterday. And she *was* romantically involved with J. J. Rahmer, who was hardly free of suspicion himself.

When she was composed enough to speak, Melanie lifted her head. "You know something funny? J.J. just got through telling me that people are going to think *I* murdered Curtis."

"Oh?" George asked, flashing an almost imperceptible glance in Nancy's direction. "Why would people think something like that?"

Swallowing hard, Melanie said, "Because I took out a three-million-dollar insurance policy on his life. It became effective the day before Curtis was killed."

At least she decided to tell us about the policy, Nancy thought, instead of trying to hide it. "That does seem a little suspicious," she said gingerly.

"I guess it does," Melanie admitted.

As the three women lapsed into silence, Nancy considered the best way to handle Melanie. The singer was either completely innocent or totally cunning—it was hard to know which.

"Why did you take out the policy, Melanie?" Nancy asked finally.

Without hesitation Melanie answered,

"Spike convinced me to do it. You know, he and I are from the same hometown. In fact, I first met Curtis through Spike. He used to be Curtis's drummer."

"So I've heard," Nancy said.

"Anyway, after he left Curtis's band, Spike was in a terrible car accident. His leg was broken in three places, and his left wrist was completely shattered. There was no way he could ever play the drums again. He didn't have one dime of insurance, either. When I went to visit him in the hospital, he told me I was crazy not to have more insurance, because you just never know what can happen. That night, when I got home, I thought over what he said, and I decided he was right. I took out a few policies the very next day—on Curtis and on myself, too."

Again Nancy had the impression that Melanie's words would be either the absolute truth or a giant lie. "Melanie," Nancy said, "the night Curtis died, you said he got a phone call that prompted him to go out. Who was it from?"

Biting her lip, Melanie shrugged helplessly. "I wish I knew who it was from," she murmured. "But Curtis wouldn't tell me. He just laughed and said he had to go smooth down some ruffled feathers and that he'd be home by eleven. I never saw him after that." Looking from Nancy to George, Melanie let out a sigh. "I don't think that call was from J.J., though, because he had called just a few hours before."

"What did J.J. call about?" George inquired.

Melanie's face clouded over. "I only heard Curtis's side of the conversation, of course. But I can tell you this—they had one of their usual spats over the phone. I remember Curtis saying, 'Now, J.J., don't go saying things you don't mean. You'd never kill anybody. And especially not me.'"

Suddenly Melanie straightened up and let out a gasp. "Oh, my," she said softly. "You don't think J.J.—?" Melanie couldn't finish the sentence.

"Are you telling us that J.J. threatened to kill Curtis the very night he died?" Nancy asked, her eyes locked into Melanie's.

"Well, yes," Melanie answered, looking dismayed. "But J.J. often said things like that when he and Curtis argued."

"Melanie, did you mention any of this to the police at the time?" Nancy asked.

Melanie thought for a moment. "I'm not sure," she said tentatively. "After all, they weren't investigating a murder, only a car accident. And, as I said, J.J. and Curtis said things like that all the time when they fought. I never took it seriously."

Just then the sound of footsteps hurrying to

the kitchen made Nancy look up toward the doorway. Spike Wilson came into the kitchen, running up to Melanie. His long brown hair hung over part of his flushed face.

"What did that jerk do to you?" he demanded. "Did he hit you? If he did, I'll—"

"Calm down, Spike," Melanie said. "What are you talking about?"

"The maid said he was shouting at you. She said she heard a crash." Spike's eyes were fixed on Melanie's surprised face at first. Then he turned and slowly took in Nancy and George.

"We were just leaving. Come on, George," Nancy said quietly. But as she turned in the direction of the kitchen entryway, she stopped and whispered to George, "Follow my lead." Then, loud enough for Melanie and Spike to hear, she said, "Wait. I think I left my notepad over there."

Grinning, George played along. "I think so, too, Nan." She followed Nancy over to a shelf with papers on it, next to a glass door that led to the garden. It was on the far end of the huge room, past the breakfast alcove. The act had been wasted on Spike and Melanie, who were so engrossed in their conversation they hadn't appeared to notice a thing.

"J.J. and I argued, that's all," Melanie was saying. "But he didn't hurt me, Spike. The crash came because I threw a vase at him. I let myself get too angry, and I lost control."

"Why is he trying to upset you when he knows you have a big performance coming up? What kind of manager would do something like that?" Spike complained.

Melanie sounded discouraged as she told Spike, "You don't understand. It's a lot more complicated than that."

"All I can see now is that he's using you," Spike broke in. "And you're letting him. Why?"

With her hand on the doorknob, Nancy stood listening to the conversation. Melanie and Spike didn't seem to realize she and George were still in the room.

Spike's voice became pleading as he added, "He's blinded you, Melanie. He's got you thinking he's the only one who can handle your career. But that's wrong, so wrong. With your talent you could have your pick of managers."

"I thought he was the best," Melanie murmured. "I know how you feel about J.J., but I still thought he was the best. Even Curtis used to say so, when he wasn't mad at him."

"Curtis is gone, Mel," Spike insisted. "And now you're letting J.J. use you. Can't you see you don't need him around?"

Nancy gave George a look that said they'd heard enough. Turning the doorknob, she hoped the door would open quietly. It swung out without a sound, and the girls slipped outside, then shut it softly behind them.

"Boy, he's sure got it bad for her," George commented, looking over at Nancy as they headed around toward the front of the house.

"So I noticed," Nancy agreed.

She paused at the edge of the garden, peering over the stone wall at the public part of Greenwood. There, hundreds of visitors were wandering in and out of the Curtis Taylor Museum and around the large white marble tombstone that marked his grave. From where the girls stood they could hear the faint sounds of piped-in music at the grave site. It was the voice of Curtis himself singing "Losing My Heart."

"Everybody seems to lose his heart to Melanie," Nancy said softly.

"Not Curtis's fans," George reminded her. "Louisa and the other die-hard Curtis fans all seem to hate her."

George paused for a moment, thinking. "Okay, so J. J. Rahmer bribed the coroner. We know that for a fact."

"Right. Go on," Nancy encouraged.

"J.J. also threatened to kill Curtis, on the very day that Curtis died."

Nancy nodded. "So Melanie says, anyway."

"All right," George said. "And obviously, despite whatever problems they may be having now, J.J. and Melanie have been romantically involved. That kiss they shared yesterday—"

"—was very convincing," Nancy agreed.

"J.J. was probably attracted to Melanie long ago," George said. "He probably figured that with Curtis out of the way, he could have her for himself. And he was right. Nancy, this case doesn't seem so complicated to me anymore. The way I figure it, J. J. Rahmer killed Curtis Taylor."

A masculine voice spoke up behind Nancy and George. "A clever deduction. Too bad it's wrong."

Spinning around, Nancy and George found themselves facing J. J. Rahmer himself.

"I agree, the evidence points to me," he said with a snide smile before Nancy could react. "That's why I just called my secretary in Nashville and had her fax up this little piece of paper."

He thrust a piece of paper into George's hand.

"It's a copy of a phone bill," George said, scanning the paper.

J. J. Rahmer nodded. "And it proves, beyond the shadow of a doubt, that I was two hundred miles away, in Lake City, the night Curtis died."

Chapter
Nine

As J. J. Rahmer watched with a superior grin, Nancy peered at the paper in George's hand. It was a copy of a hotel bill from five years ago, made out to Rahmer, with the telephone charge marked on it. Nancy recognized Greenwood's phone number from the card Tyrone had given her.

"I've found it pays to keep records," J.J. said in a self-congratulatory tone.

It looks as though he has an ironclad alibi, Nancy thought. But she still had questions that needed answers. "Then why did you bribe Dexter Mobley to change the coroner's report about the barbiturates found in Curtis's blood the night he died?" she asked. "We have very strong proof that you paid Mobley off."

The smug look fell from Rahmer's face, replaced by a cold, hard stare. "Aren't you girls awfully young to be investigators?"

Ignoring Rahmer's sneer, Nancy challenged, "Why did you bribe him? We know it cost you plenty, so you must have had a very good reason."

"That's for me to know and you to find out," he muttered, striding away toward the mansion.

Nancy decided to take a wild chance. "Or did you do it to protect someone else?" she called out just loudly enough for him to hear. "Melanie, for instance?"

Rahmer stopped in his tracks. Even George looked surprised by Nancy's suggestion. Daggers seemed to flash out of Rahmer's eyes as he looked over his shoulder at them.

"That's quite an accusation!" he shouted, shaking a finger at them. "Let me tell you ladies something. No jury on earth would condemn a manager who was trying to protect his client's good reputation—even if those actions went a little beyond the letter of the law. All I'd have to say is that I was trying to spare the public the heartbreak of knowing that their squeaky-clean Curtis was secretly a druggie. The most any jury would give me is a slap on the wrist."

Nancy watched as Rahmer continued toward the house with long, angry strides.

"That's an excitable man," George murmured.

"I'll say," Nancy agreed. "Come on. Let's talk about all this while we drive back to Louisa's." She checked her watch. "It's already after three. The party at the Imperial will probably be over soon, anyway."

As Nancy inched the car through the heavy traffic outside the security gate, George turned to her and said, "That was weird. I mean, J.J. definitely reacted when you suggested he was trying to cover up for Melanie. But when we talked to her, she seemed so sincere."

Nancy tried to sort through the jumbled thoughts in her head. "That could have been an act. Without more proof we can't know why he paid the coroner to change the report. It could have been to protect Melanie, or himself, or to protect Curtis Taylor's image, the way J.J. claimed."

"I guess you're right," George said.

Stopping the car at a red light, Nancy said, "I can't help thinking that the romantic angle has something to do with this case, too. I mean, J.J. and Melanie are together, and—

"Do you think J.J. and Melanie could have planned Curtis's murder together?" George interrupted suddenly. "Maybe they were in love while Curtis was still alive. Just because

J.J. has an alibi for the night of the murder doesn't mean he didn't help plan it."

"Maybe. The song Curtis wrote *is* about her being with another guy," Nancy said, thinking out loud. "And then there's Spike, too. He has it bad for Melanie." She shook her head ruefully. "I just can't figure out how it all fits together. We still don't have enough proof to know anything for sure."

George leaned back in the passenger seat and grinned at Nancy. "Well, I know one thing for sure. We've got to give our brains a rest. Tonight we're getting to see the dress rehearsal of the hottest country-western show in the whole U.S.A. So for just a little while, let's stop trying to figure out who was after Curtis Taylor and concentrate on having a good time instead."

Loud Curtis Taylor music was pouring out the open windows of Louisa's house when Nancy and George drove up. Walking in the unlocked door, they heard Bess and Louisa singing along at the top of their lungs on the upper level of the house.

"Hi, you two!" Nancy called up the stairs when the song was over.

"How was the party?" George asked.

"Nancy, George, you're home!" Bess cried, galloping down the stairs. "The party was great. I now have the autographs of Billy

Rutteridge, Malcolm Coleman, and every one of the Blue Mountain Boys," she said proudly.

Louisa appeared on the stairs behind Bess, wearing a checked robe and a huge smile. "Are you two hungry?" she asked. "Bess and I ate so much at that party that we're both stuffed. But there's some macaroni and cheese that you can heat up in the microwave."

"Thanks," George said. "We never did get to eat lunch, and I'm starved."

As they all went into the kitchen, Louisa's face took on a more serious look. "How did *your* day go? Find out anything?"

"Whew," Nancy answered. "Did we ever. Tell them, George."

While Nancy fixed herself and George a couple of plates, George filled Louisa and Bess in on everything they'd learned about Melanie, J.J., and Spike.

"Seems to me," Louisa said when George was finished, "that you've learned more about Curtis's death in a few days than the police learned in five years."

Nancy laughed. "That's not quite fair, Louisa," she pointed out. "Remember, the police weren't even aware that there was anything to look for. They never saw the song or heard the tape."

Propping her elbows on the kitchen table, Bess said, "Poor Tyrone. He has to live with Melanie and J.J. Do you think they might try to hurt him because he's looking into Curtis's death?"

"I hope not," Nancy told her.

"Uh-oh," Louisa said, pointing at the kitchen clock over her sink. "We'd better get ready. It's only one hour to showtime, and there's bound to be a lot of traffic tonight."

Half an hour later Louisa, Nancy, and George were back in the front hall.

"Come on, Bess," George called up the stairs, smoothing her red sweater dress. Nancy and Louisa were waiting with her by the door, Nancy in a brown leather skirt and silky white blouse, and Louisa in a belted green dress.

A moment later Bess joined them, wearing a black silk jumpsuit. "Okay, I'm ready," she announced.

"We can take my car," Nancy said as they stepped out of the house.

Ten minutes later, when Nancy turned onto one of Maywood's main drags, she found herself in the biggest traffic jam she had experienced since the last time she'd been in New York City. "Oh, no," she moaned. "We'll never get there on time."

Louisa leaned forward from the backseat, a mischievous gleam in her eye. "I haven't lived in Maywood fifteen years for nothing," she said. "Take a left up by that doughnut shop."

"You mean that little alley?" Nancy asked.

"That's right. This town is filled with shortcuts, if you know where they are," Louisa said, flashing a knowing smile.

Nancy squeezed her car out of the traffic and through the alley. After she'd dodged a couple of Dumpsters, she pulled onto a nearly empty street. "Just go down the hill here and under the railroad trestle. We'll come out by the loading dock of the Civic Center."

"Ha!" Nancy cried triumphantly as Louisa's directions led them exactly where she'd said they would. "Louisa, you're a genius."

It took them another ten minutes to get into the parking lot and find a spot, but Nancy saw that they still had a few minutes before the show was due to start. They joined the stream of people who were invited to the rehearsal as they flowed toward the Civic Center. Nancy was filled with excitement. Not only was she going to see a great concert once, but she'd have a chance to see the same performers the next night.

Inside, Nancy and her friends took their seats, which were in the ninth row, as the house lights faded to black. The only light in the hall was the brilliant yellow radiating from the stage lights.

Rambling Rosie Rodgers, a comedian, was the first act on the bill. She warmed the crowd up with her funny jokes, which were punctuated by harmonica music.

After Rambling Rosie came Billy Rutteridge, singing a musical tribute to Curtis. Rutteridge was followed by the Blue Mountain Boys, who did a medley of bluegrass music.

"They're fantastic!" Nancy yelled to Bess over the audience's loud cheering. "I've got to get one of their albums."

The cheers faded when Melanie Taylor stepped center stage for her first number, "Losing My Heart." The moving strains of the piano introduction came, and then her smooth voice glided into the music.

Nancy noticed that even Louisa was enraptured by her singing. By the time Melanie finished three numbers, Nancy suspected she had made more than a few new fans—namely, everybody in the audience.

"Tyrone is on after this," Bess said excitedly as the crowd cheered for Melanie. "Wait till you see his neon guitar light up."

There was no time for Nancy to remind Bess that she'd already seen the special-effect instrument, so Nancy just leaned back in her seat, ready to enjoy the act.

Tyrone looked fantastic in the gold lamé cowboy outfit, Nancy thought. As he played the opening bars of "Loose as a Goose," Tyrone swooped and jumped with the guitar from one side of the stage to the other. Colorful sparkles of light shot out everywhere from the guitar.

"Oh, I'm loose as a goose, as a goose on the loose. I was caught in a noose, but——"

Suddenly Tyrone gave an agonized, guttural cry that made Nancy flinch. In an instant smoke was pouring from the guitar as sparks flew around Tyrone. The singer writhed in agony, trying to disengage himself from the instrument.

"Oh, no!" Nancy exclaimed, grabbing Bess's arm. "Tyrone's being electrocuted!"

Chapter

Ten

NANCY WATCHED IN HORROR as Tyrone collapsed on the stage floor.

"Help him!" Bess shrieked, jumping to her feet. "Somebody help him!" Other people around the girls started moving from their seats, surging forward to get a closer look at the stricken performer.

Onstage two men with hand-held fire extinguishers appeared, smothering the flames in a steaming mist. Several other people approached Tyrone, circling him, but not touching him. They seemed to be anxiously awaiting someone else—a doctor, Nancy presumed.

"Ladies and gentlemen," a disembodied voice echoed through the hall. Nancy guessed it was someone from the management talking from the sound booth above the arena. "Please remain in your seats and stay calm. Mr. Taylor will be attended to immediately. Meanwhile, we ask you to be patient. In a few minutes we'll announce whether the rehearsal will proceed as planned. Thank you."

That announcement had some effect on the crowd, and Nancy was relieved to see that most people did as instructed.

"I'm going up there," Bess said, pushing her way past Louisa and George, out into the aisle.

"Bess, no," George said, grabbing hold of her sleeve. "You can't do anything for him now. You'll only get in the way."

Just then a man carrying a black medical bag ran onto the stage toward Tyrone. The people around the singer made space, and the doctor knelt beside Tyrone, checking for vital signs.

"Oh, good, a doctor's there now," Bess said in a small voice, her blue eyes filled with tears.

With a wave of his arm the doctor summoned two large men carrying a stretcher. An audible cry of relief went through the crowd as Nancy and the others noticed Tyrone move slightly. Seconds later he was rushed off the stage on the stretcher.

"I've got to find out where they're taking him," Bess said, getting up again and hurrying down the aisle toward the stage.

Cupping her hands around her mouth, Louisa called after Bess. "Probably to Maywood Medical Center. It's the closest hospital." But Bess didn't seem to hear.

"Let's go with Bess," Nancy said, turning to George. "I want to check out a few things onstage." She reached for her car keys and gave them to Louisa. "Would you mind bringing my car around back to the loading dock and waiting there?" she asked.

When Louisa gave her a quizzical look, Nancy explained, "They're definitely going to cancel this concert, and I want to be able to leave for the hospital before the crowd pours out of here."

Hurrying down the red-carpeted aisle, Nancy and George caught up with Bess near the edge of the stage, talking to a security guard.

"He's already on his way to Maywood Medical Center," Bess informed Nancy and George. "Come on, let's go."

But Nancy and George held back. "Louisa's bringing the car around to the loading dock to wait for us, but I need to look around the stage first," Nancy said in a low voice so the guard wouldn't hear. "Do you see anyone who might let us up there?"

Grinning, Bess fished around in her bag and pulled out a pass that read Stage Crew— Curtis Taylor Five-Year Memorial Gala. "I saved this from when I worked with Tyrone yesterday. She showed the pass to the guard, who immediately let the girls up the short set of steps that led to the stage.

"Hey!" a burly man from the crew shouted when he noticed the girls were about to step onstage. "No one's allowed—"

But he stopped the minute Bess looked up. "Oh, it's you. Come on up, Bess."

"These girls are with me, Frank," Bess explained. "Where's the nearest exit to the loading dock from here?"

The stagehand pointed across the backstage area. "Back past those backdrops, over by the wall—you'll see a door."

"Thanks," Bess said. Looking expectantly at Nancy, she asked, "What do you want to check out?"

"You and George look around and see if you can find out where J.J. and Melanie are," Nancy told her. "Meanwhile, I want to check out this equipment."

Nancy stepped close to the place where Tyrone's guitar lay on the floor, then followed the charred cables across the stage.

"Spike," she said, practically bumping into the long-haired former drummer where the wires crossed into the backstage area. "What are you doing here?"

Curtis Taylor's former drummer was leaning against the backstage wall, his hands shoved in the pockets of his pants. "What are *you* doing here?" he shot back. "I've been coming here off and on since this circus came to town. I've got a lot of old pals I like to hang out with, do you mind?"

"It was just a question," Nancy said. When he walked away, she stared after him for a moment, then continued following the cables.

Behind a trunk filled with unused stage equipment, Nancy found what she was looking for. A section of two cables was taped together. Carefully unwrapping the silver tape, which was still hot to the touch, she saw that the cables had been stripped of their insulation. A deliberate short circuit if there ever was one, Nancy thought.

She looked excitedly around for Bess and George. A moment later she spotted them hurrying toward her from the stage's left wing.

"Well, J.J. and Melanie were both here," Bess told Nancy. "We saw Eddie—you remember, the guy George was dancing with at that party? Anyway, he said J.J. was in Melanie's dressing room for an hour before the show, and they had a huge fight. Eddie heard her say she wanted to break off the relationship, personal *and* business. When he asked why, she told him she was in love with another man."

"Eddie didn't hear her say who it was, though," George added.

Nancy blew out a breath as this new information sank in. "Spike is here, too, which means that any of our suspects could have been the one who did this." She gestured to where the wires had been bared and taped together.

"He could have been killed!" Bess gasped. "Whoever did that deserves to be locked up."

With a firm nod Nancy said, "That's exactly what I intend to do. Come on, you guys. I want to show this to a security guard. And then let's go to the hospital."

A large group of people were assembled at the hospital in the visitors' waiting area. Among them were photographers and reporters, even a videotape crew.

Melanie was there, too, Nancy saw. The singer was still wearing the glittery outfit she'd performed in earlier. Her usually pretty face looked tired and drawn as she slumped down in one of the turquoise vinyl chairs lining the waiting room.

Looking around, Nancy's eyes were drawn to the other side of the room, where a gray-haired man sat in a corner, wearing slacks, a knit turtleneck, and a beige cap.

"Vickers," she called out, going over to him. Bess, George, and Louisa were right behind her. "I almost didn't recognize you without your uniform."

"Good evening, ladies," he said quietly. "Tonight was my night off, so I thought I'd take in the dress rehearsal." With a miserable shake of his head the butler added, "It certainly didn't turn out to be a very festive occasion."

Just then one of the doors marked Authorized Personnel Only swung open, and a well-dressed young woman wearing a white lab jacket stepped in front of the assembled crowd. "I have an announcement," she said in a loud voice.

Nancy and her friends stepped closer to her. As videotape crews flashed on their lights, the woman began reading from a clipboard. "Half an hour ago Mr. Tyrone Taylor was admitted to this center, the victim of a severe electrical shock, which he received in an accident during a performance this evening. Mr. Taylor is alive, but his condition is quite serious. Our staff will report to you again in one hour. Thank you." With that, she turned on her heel and pushed back through the swinging door.

"At least he's alive," Bess murmured as George threw a comforting arm around her cousin's shoulders.

"Do you think we should stay here or go home?" Louisa asked the girls.

"Stay here, of course," Bess answered.

Shrugging, George said, "Whatever you all want to do . . ."

With the case still unsolved, Nancy wasn't sure whether to stay at the hospital or leave.

She had a feeling that Tyrone's accident was connected to Curtis Taylor's death, that whoever had killed Curtis was sending Tyrone and Nancy a strong message to back off the case. And that meant it was extremely urgent that she find Curtis Taylor's killer as quickly as possible.

The case had been frustrating so far. Since Curtis had died five years earlier, it wasn't as if there was still any concrete evidence lying around.

Or was there?

Nancy's head snapped up suddenly. "You guys, I just thought of something. Remember what Vickers said about the formal living room being unchanged since the night Curtis died?"

Louisa, Bess, and George all nodded.

"Well, I was thinking about that. Melanie told the coroner that Curtis had one bourbon every night at eight," Nancy went on. "If he was killed, maybe there's some clue in that bar we saw in the formal living room."

"Sounds like a long shot," George put in doubtfully, "but I'll go with you to check it out if you want."

Nancy noticed Vickers getting up to leave. Calling over to him, she asked, "Would you mind giving us a lift to Greenwood? There are a few things I'd like to look at over there."

"Of course, Miss Drew," he answered.

After making arrangements for Bess and Louisa to pick them up at the estate in an hour and a half, Nancy and George left with the butler.

Half an hour later the girls found themselves alone in Greenwood's formal living room, where Nancy made a beeline for the bar.

"Melanie told the coroner that Curtis had one bourbon every night at eight." She searched through the row of colored glass decanters until she found the one marked Bourbon. Uncorking it, she sniffed inside the bottle. "It doesn't smell very strong."

George walked over to the bar and handed Nancy a glass from a nearby hanging rack. "Pour some," she suggested.

"I thought bourbon was a kind of orange color," George said, staring skeptically at the clear liquid Nancy had poured into the glass. "Maybe that's gin or vodka. They're both clear, like water."

After dipping her finger into the glass and tasting it, Nancy raised an eyebrow. "This *is* water."

"Do the other decanters all have water in them, too?" George asked, uncapping them one at a time.

A simple sniff was all the answer either of them needed. "These are all full of the real thing," Nancy said.

"Which means—?" George began.

"Somebody tampered with this decanter," Nancy concluded. "Probably the same person who put barbiturates in it for Curtis to drink."

"So whoever killed Curtis Taylor had to have access to the formal living room in order to come back and get rid of the evidence after Curtis's death."

Nancy nodded, walking distractedly over to one of the living room windows. Her brow knit in concentration as she stared out over the grounds.

"Melanie Taylor, J. J. Rahmer, and Spike Wilson," she murmured, letting her eyes rove over the public part of the estate, now dark except for a few security lights. "Which one did it?"

"Hey, Nan, look," George said, walking up beside her and leaning closer to the window. "Someone's down there."

Focusing more sharply, Nancy glimpsed a shadowy figure swinging something down by Curtis Taylor's memorial.

"I can't believe it," she gasped a moment later. "Someone's out there trying to smash Curtis's gravestone!"

Chapter
Eleven

"COME ON!" Nancy cried, running toward the kitchen. There was a door there that led out to the formal gardens, she remembered. That seemed like the most direct way to the public part of the estate.

"Vickers, call the security guards right away!" she exclaimed when she saw the butler reading the newspaper at the kitchen table. "Better tell them to contact the police, too!"

George was right behind Nancy as she flew across the lawn and past the gardens. In seconds large floodlights blinked on, spilling bright light all over the public part of the estate. The separating wall was down the knoll from Nancy and George, and Nancy was able to glimpse a shadowy form run into the trees. In the glare of the emergency lights, she could also make out a large gash in the neck of the marble guitar-shaped statue next to Curtis Taylor's tombstone.

Soon Vickers joined them outside. "I hope the security staff was able to catch the culprit," he said.

"Let's go find out," Nancy suggested. "How do we get past that wall?"

Vickers held up a key and instructed, "Follow me."

As they headed toward the wall, Nancy looked around in every direction, hoping to catch a better look at the shadowy figure. But she saw nothing.

Vickers led her and George to a heavy iron gate in the wall, took out his key, and hurriedly opened it. From there the three entered the public part of the property. Walking over to the damaged tombstone, Nancy saw a few security officers checking over the marble structure. Another couple of guards were searching the nearby trees and bushes.

"Did you see who it was?" Nancy asked one of the guards.

The guard shook her head. "I saw someone running away, but I couldn't make out much about him," she replied, shining her flashlight in the branches of a large oak tree.

"Him? You mean it was a man?" George asked.

Looking confused, the guard admitted, "Well, it could have been a woman, I suppose."

Nancy turned as another security guard emerged from a wooded lot on the edge of the tombstone area, holding a sledgehammer. He had a handkerchief carefully wrapped around it. "I found this by the bushes near the road," he told the female guard. "We can give it to the police to dust for prints. Looks like our guy got away, though."

Seeing George inspecting the damaged statue, Nancy went over to join her.

"Who would do something like this?" George asked, shaking her head in disbelief. "Who would hate Curtis Taylor's memory enough to want to smash up his memorial statue?"

"Maybe the same person who hated him enough to kill him," Nancy replied. "If it was, I just hope we can catch the person before anything or anyone else gets hurt."

"Tyrone is going to be okay," Bess informed Nancy and George when she and Louisa picked them up at Greenwood later.

Steering Nancy's car past the security gate and onto the road, Louisa added, "They've postponed the concert till Sunday, though, to give him a chance to recover."

"You won't believe what happened here," George said, leaning forward to rest her hands on the back of the passenger seat. She told Bess and Louisa about the vandalized tombstone and finding water in the bourbon decanter.

"Why would anyone do something like that?" Louisa asked with a horrified gasp. "I just don't get it."

"Who would do it? That's what I'd like to know," Bess added from the passenger seat.

Nancy had been mulling over that same question. "Well, it couldn't have been Melanie," she pointed out. "She was at the hospital, right?"

Bess nodded. "She was there the whole time. She seemed really concerned about Tyrone, too."

"That leaves J.J. and Spike unaccounted for, though," George noted. "Unless it was just some random prank, which I find pretty unlikely, considering all that's been going on lately."

Louisa shot Nancy an uneasy look in the rearview mirror. "Are you any closer to finding out who killed Curtis?" she asked worriedly.

Letting out a sigh, Nancy admitted, "Not really."

They drove the rest of the way in silence. "It must be after midnight already," Louisa said, turning into her driveway. She shut off the motor and reached for the car door handle.

"Ten after," George said, glancing at her watch with a yawn. "Come on, guys. I'm going to turn in."

"I'm tired, too," Nancy said after she got out of the car. She started walking up to Louisa's front door.

"Aunt Louisa, want me to take this mail in?" Bess asked. In front of her a white envelope stuck out of Louisa's brass mailbox, which was on the wall to the right of the front door. "Or did you put it there for the carrier to pick up?"

With a puzzled look on her face, Louisa reached into the mailbox. "That's funny," she said. "I got my mail this afternoon."

"It's probably just an ad," Bess said.

Holding the envelope close to her eyes, Louisa peered through her glasses at it. "No, it's not," she said. "It's an envelope. For Nancy. Someone must have brought it by while we were out. Do you know anybody else in Maywood, Nancy?"

"No," Nancy said, taking the envelope from Louisa. Sure enough, her name was clearly printed on the front.

"Let's see what this is about," Nancy murmured, ripping open the envelope.

Under the glare of the porch light she took

out a letter and unfolded it. But her breath caught in her throat when she read the brief message:

Nancy Drew, stop digging up dirt. You might wind up under six feet of it.

Chapter
Twelve

"Nan?" George asked in a worried voice. "Everything okay?"

For a second Nancy didn't know what to say. Finally she handed the note to George, who read it with a look of shock on her face.

"Let's go in," Nancy said when George was finished.

Louisa opened the door, and the four women stepped into the house. Bess flicked on the hall light, saying to George, "Let me see that." Lifting the paper out of George's hands, she read it aloud.

"Oh, no!" Louisa cried. "How awful."

Bess's hands were shaking as she handed the note back to Nancy. "First Tyrone, then Curtis's tombstone, and now this," she murmured.

"That note is a murder threat, Nan, pure and simple," George added. "What are you going to do about it?"

Nancy tapped the folded note with her finger. "I'll definitely call the police about it tomorrow morning," she promised.

Her mind was racing as she tried to reconstruct what had happened. "Whoever left that note left it while we were gone," she surmised, following the others into the living room and flopping down on the sofa next to Louisa.

"Curtis's killer must be awfully afraid we're closing in on him if he tried to electrocute Tyrone and threatened to kill you all in one day," Bess said, frowning. "Nan, we just can't let him get away with this."

Wringing her hands, Louisa gave Nancy a distressed look. "You know, I hate to say this, but maybe you girls should pack up and head back to River Heights tomorrow. Not that I want you to go—I don't. But you might be better off just forgetting all about this nasty business."

Nancy shook her head firmly. "There's no way I'm leaving until I find out who killed Curtis Taylor."

"We're with you all the way, Nan," George told her with a grin.

Louisa still looked worried. "Curtis is already dead," she pointed out. "But if anything happens to you girls, I'll never forgive myself."

Leveling her serious blue eyes at Louisa, Nancy said, "We'll be very careful. Nothing bad will happen, I promise."

Nancy just hoped it was a promise that could be kept.

The next morning Nancy woke up before any of her friends. After phoning the police and telling them about the note, she headed into the kitchen to make herself breakfast.

Let me just make sure I haven't received any other strange messages during the night, she thought as she measured water into the coffee machine. Nancy went to the front door and peeked out but was relieved to see that the mailbox was empty. At her feet was the day's edition of the *Maywood Morning Star.*

"Tyrone Taylor Murder Attempt" read the largest headline. Under it, in smaller letters, was "Narrow Escape for Budding Star." To the left was a copy of Tyrone's photo as he appeared on the cover of the *Heartthrob* cassette.

Nancy brought the paper into the kitchen and spread it out on the table to read.

"What's that?" Bess asked when she wandered down in her bathrobe a few minutes later, yawning and rubbing her eyes. "Isn't that Tyrone's picture? What does it say?" she asked, suddenly alert.

As Bess poured herself some coffee, Nancy recapped the article's main points. "It just tells about the accident onstage, and that police suspect someone tampered with the electrical system—nothing we don't already know."

"What's happening?" George asked as she and Louisa came into the kitchen, already dressed. Seeing the newspaper, George asked, "Does it say anything about the tombstone vandalism?"

Nancy flipped through the pages of the paper. "I don't see anything about that," she said. "I guess it happened too late to be included in the early edition."

Nancy was impatient to begin work on the case, but she wanted to give everyone a chance to wake up first. Once they had finished their muffins, coffee, and tea, Nancy turned to Louisa and Bess and said, "I was wondering if you two have any time to do a little investigating for me today."

"Sure, Nancy," Bess said. "What do you want us to do?"

"I have all day," Louisa said. With a sigh she added, "Especially now that the gala has been postponed until tomorrow."

Nancy propped her elbows on the table and rested her chin in her hands. "You know the crew of the gala the best of any of us, Bess," she said. "I'd like you to ask around and see if someone noticed anything unusual backstage before last night's performance. Also, any information you can find about J. J. Rahmer's whereabouts after the concert would be important to have. Louisa, you can help Bess get around, okay?"

Louisa and Bess both nodded. "Just one thing, Nan," Bess said. "I want to go see Tyrone today, too."

"No problem," Nancy said. "George and I will meet you at the hospital later."

Smiling at Nancy, George asked, "So what are we going to do?"

"I want to bounce ideas off you, if that's okay, George."

After Louisa and Bess had left, Nancy found Louisa's collection of Curtis Taylor clippings and spread them on the coffee table in the living room. Next to them she placed the cassette tape with Curtis's message and the one of Tyrone's rendition of "Melanie," the paper that the song was written on, Curtis's letter, as well as the threatening note she'd received the night before.

"I don't even know where to start, George," she confessed as she sat down on a throw pillow on the floor, leaning over the table. "But sometimes it's best to go back to the beginning. Tyrone gave me a bunch of stuff that I've hardly had a chance to look over."

"Let's listen to the song," George suggested.

She picked up the cassette and popped it into Louisa's tape deck. Then she stretched out on the sofa to listen.

On came Tyrone, doing his best to present the song "Melanie."

"You left me, and now you're with him.
Someday he'll be gone, though,
and your heart I'll win. . . ."

"Those lyrics are just so bad," George groaned. "Maybe he asked his dentist to write it for him?"

Nancy froze in the middle of her giggle. "George," she said softly, "you know what? You might have something there." Her heart pumping furiously, Nancy looked at the sheet music for "Melanie," studying the handwriting. Then she jumped up and walked over to look at the writing on the autographed picture of Curtis Taylor over Louisa's sofa.

"Brilliant, George!" Nancy cried. "You're absolutely brilliant."

"I am?" George said, looking confused.

Pointing at the framed picture on Louisa's wall, Nancy exclaimed, "Look right there! When Curtis autographed this picture for Louisa, he wrote the words *Best wishes* in block print."

Nancy held the song sheet up to the framed

photo, and George stepped over to get a better look. "They look about the same to me, Nan," George said.

"That's because most block printing looks alike. But don't you see it, George? If you look closely, the printing on Curtis's picture is distinctly different from the lyrics printed on the sheet of music!"

Her eyes went from Curtis Taylor's framed photo to the lyrics for "Melanie" in her hand. "Look at these *W*'s. When Curtis wrote them, he rounded the bottoms. But the ones on the lyrics are jagged."

George nodded, comparing the two pieces of writing. "I see what you mean, Nan," she murmured.

"And check out the *T*'s," Nancy added. "The tops of Curtis's are high up, and the ones in the song lyrics are much lower."

Nancy's eyes sparkled with excitement as she concluded, "Curtis Taylor didn't write 'Melanie.'"

Chapter

Thirteen

B UT IF Curtis didn't write 'Melanie,' then who did?" George asked.

"That's a good question," Nancy commented, rereading the lyrics. "'You left me, and now you're with him.' So it's someone Melanie left, obviously."

Nancy went back over to the coffee table and picked up the threatening note she'd gotten the night before. She held it in one hand and the sheet music to "Melanie" in the other. "The same block letters, George," she said, drawing in her breath sharply. "Look."

"But whose are they, Nan?"

"That's what we've got to find out," Nancy said. She put down the song lyric and started for the kitchen phone but stopped herself in midstride. "No, we'd better handle this in person."

Confusion was written all over George's face as she looked at Nancy. "Handle what?"

"Come on, George. We're going to dig up a skeleton," Nancy informed her. "A skeleton in Melanie Taylor's closet."

When they arrived at Greenwood, Vickers directed Nancy and George out to the formal gardens. "She's been out there for almost an hour, watching while they work on the statue by Mr. Taylor's tombstone," he said with a frown. "Needless to say, the grounds are closed to the public today."

"Thanks, Vickers," Nancy said.

Melanie was standing on the lawn in a full-length black leather coat, gazing over the wall to where a group of workers were removing the guitar-shaped statue from the tombstone area below. As Nancy and George approached, Nancy saw that the singer was biting her lip and blinking back tears.

"Melanie," Nancy said softly. "Can we talk? It's important."

The beautiful singer nodded sadly, her eyes still on the workers below. Finally she looked at Nancy and George and said, "Why don't we go back inside, where it's warm."

When they all were in the living room, Melanie collapsed into a chair. "I'm such a wreck," she confided. "This business with Tyrone, and then the gravestone. Isn't it horrible?"

Nancy looked directly into the singer's cool gray eyes as she and George sat down on a brocade loveseat. "I want to bring all this trouble to an end, Melanie, but I need your help. Are you willing?"

"Yes, I suppose so," Melanie said, shifting uncomfortably in her chair.

"Your love life before you met Curtis," Nancy began. "Can you tell us about it?"

Melanie seemed momentarily taken aback. "What about it?" she said with a shrug. "I've —I've had my share of boyfriends, I suppose."

"Was one of them a songwriter, by any chance?" George asked.

"A songwriter? I don't think so. . . ." Melanie seemed lost in thought.

"J. J. Rahmer never wrote songs, as far as you know?" Nancy pressed her.

Looking confused, Melanie replied, "Not that I know of."

"Maybe we can ask him about it ourselves," George suggested. "Will he be around today?"

Melanie let out a sudden laugh. "Honey, I'm afraid J.J. won't be around here today or any other day."

"Oh?" Nancy asked, puzzled.

"He went off to Nashville early last night, before Tyrone's accident," Melanie explained. "And he's never coming back."

With a look of conviction in her eyes, she explained, "We broke up for good last night. I finally realized that Curtis was right about J.J. all along. Oh, at first, when I was trying to launch my career, I thought I needed J.J. For a while there I guess I got love and need all mixed up. But lately, I've come to see what a snake that man was. He wanted me to sign a contract that gave all the advantage to him and none to me. And worst of all, he thought I was a killer!"

Nancy and George exchanged an almost imperceptible look. They certainly weren't going to tell Melanie that practically everyone who knew Curtis had been murdered thought she might be the killer.

"Would you mind if we use your phone to confirm that your manager left?" Nancy asked Melanie. "Not many planes would have left Maywood for Nashville last night."

Melanie nodded. "Sure. You can use the phone in the kitchen."

"I'll go, Nan," George said, getting up from the couch.

When George was gone, Nancy asked Melanie, "Are you sure none of your boyfriends was a songwriter? What about Spike?"

"Spike?" Melanie echoed, looking startled. "Well, yes, Spike does write songs. But—"

"Take a look at this, then," Nancy cut in, pulling the folded-up song lyric out of her purse. "Could this have been written by Spike?"

Melanie's eyes scanned the sheet. "I suppose so," she said tentatively. "There's just one problem. Spike was never my boyfriend. Never."

"Oh?"

"He and I are just friends, that's all. Oh, I suppose there was a time before I met Curtis . . ." She stared into the distance, going back to that time in her mind. "I didn't have a boyfriend, and Spike took me out to dinner a few times. But I never took it very seriously. It was more like we were just buddies, as far as I was concerned. Then Spike got a job with Curtis's band, and when he introduced me to Curtis, I knew I'd met the man I wanted to spend my life with."

" 'You left me, and now you're with him. Someday he'll be gone, though, and your heart I'll win. . . .' " Nancy said slowly. "How did Spike react when you wound up with J. J. Rahmer, Melanie?"

"Not very well," Melanie confessed. "But last night, when I told him that J.J. and I were finished, he didn't react very well, either."

That was odd, thought Nancy. She would

have expected Spike to be ecstatic. She hesitated, unsure of how to phrase her next question. "Didn't you tell J.J. that you were in love with another man?" Nancy challenged.

Melanie looked sharply at Nancy for a moment. "I guess somebody overheard us fighting, huh? We weren't exactly being quiet about it."

"And who is that other man, Melanie? The one you said you were in love with. It's important that I know."

"Why, it's Curtis," Melanie said at once, her eyes filling with tears. "That's what I told Spike, too." She heaved a heavy sigh and added, "I guess Spike's always been sort of sweet on me."

Just then George came back. "J.J. left town last night, all right," she told Nancy. "At nine-thirty. He couldn't have damaged that tombstone, Nan."

Nancy looked at George and said excitedly, "George, it's all starting to come together. Spike Wilson used to write songs, and he's been in love with Melanie for years."

"But, Nancy, Spike couldn't possibly have killed Curtis," Melanie protested. "Everybody knows he was out in the county hospital, way out on Route four fifty-nine. And he was all banged up—"

"Route four fifty-nine!" Nancy exclaimed.

"Say no more." Putting her hand on Melanie's shoulder, Nancy added gently, "I'm sorry if anything we said today was upsetting, but you have to understand, we're talking about murder."

Melanie nodded and let out a big sigh. "I know," she said softly. "And don't worry about me. I'll be okay."

"Good," Nancy answered. "Come on, George. We've got to visit the county hospital."

"I'm convinced that Spike is the one who called Curtis the night he died," Nancy said as she and George drove to the hospital.

Shaking her head doubtfully, George said, "But how could Spike possibly have left the hospital, put the poison in Curtis's decanter, and come back—all with casts on his arm and leg?"

"All I know," Nancy said, "is that people who commit murder can be highly motivated. You know that old saying, 'Where there's a will, there's a way'? We've got to find out what that way was."

Fifteen minutes later Nancy pulled into the hospital parking lot and stopped her car in an empty spot. "I wish I could look into the hospital's file on Spike, but I'm sure all the records are kept confidential."

"Where should we start, Nan?" George asked as they walked across the lot.

"Let's try the cafeteria," Nancy suggested. "People sometimes have time to talk when they're there."

The girls entered the hospital's lobby, where a nurse at the reception desk directed them to a second-floor cafeteria. Walking with their trays of danishes and tea, Nancy saw a large table where three nurses sat, relaxing. One of them was reading the *Maywood Morning Star*.

Nancy nodded in their direction. "They look friendly," she said quietly.

Approaching the table, George broke into a smile. "Okay if we sit here?" she asked.

"Sure, pull up a chair," a thin, red-haired nurse told her.

After they sat down, Nancy glanced over at the newspaper. "Excuse me," she said, feigning surprise. "Is that something about Tyrone Taylor?"

The nurse looked up from the paper and over at Nancy. "Didn't you hear? He had a bad accident last night. Someone tried to kill him."

"Wow," Nancy said, reading the paper that the nurse pushed closer to her. "He's Curtis Taylor's nephew, isn't he?"

Giving Nancy a look, one of the other nurses said, "You must be from out of town. Everyone here knows the Taylors."

"We are. We were just visiting our uncle here in the hospital," George fibbed.

"I'm a big Curtis Taylor fan, though," Nancy added quickly. "I have all his records. In fact, didn't I read that one of his band members was once here in this hospital?"

The red-haired nurse considered that for a moment. "She means Spike Wilson, right, Mary?"

"That's right," the nurse with the newspaper agreed with a nod.

"Really? Curtis Taylor's drummer? Did you get to meet him?" Nancy asked eagerly.

"No, not me," the woman answered, turning to her companions. "Who was his nurse? Was it Donna Johnson?"

"Boy, I'd love to talk to her," Nancy said. "I wonder what he was really like."

Unfortunately, Donna Johnson was still on her shift, but the nurses assured Nancy and George that she would be down for a break soon. After what seemed like forever, the red-haired nurse spotted Donna and called her over.

Donna Johnson had graying brown hair and bright hazel eyes. "Hi, everybody," she said, walking over with her tray and sitting down.

"These girls were asking about Spike Wilson," the nurse named Mary said.

It took Donna a minute to remember, but

then she laughed and said, "Oh, what a character. The guy had a foot and a hand in a cast, and we still couldn't hold him down."

"Really?" Nancy said, acting as though she were a delighted fan.

"One morning I came in to check his blood pressure, and he was gone," the nurse said. "He'd put pillows in his bed to make it look like he was sleeping. We searched everywhere for him."

George had been listening with an expression of rapt attention on her face. "Where was he?"

"Beats me," Donna said with a shrug. "When I saw him later that afternoon, he was sitting on his bed, acting as if nothing had happened."

George fiddled with her empty cup, asking, "Wasn't that around the time Curtis died?"

As soon as the words were out of George's mouth, the older nurse turned serious. "Curtis died that very night," Donna said. "Oh, that was terrible. Spike felt awful about it, too. Not only that, his leg was all swollen from his little adventure. We had to put him in a wheelchair and give him extra sedation just to get him to the funeral. He insisted on going."

Nancy's ears perked up. "Extra sedation? What did you sedate him with?"

"At that time we used to give liquid barbiturates. He'd been on them for weeks, what with the problems he had from his accident. Hey, where are you going?"

Nancy and George were already halfway to the door. "I forgot!" Nancy cried over her shoulder. "We're supposed to meet some friends."

As the two girls hurried out of the hospital, Nancy was filled with a sense of triumph.

"Yes!" she cried excitedly. "Spike *could* have poisoned Curtis's decanter of bourbon with liquid barbiturates. Spike was clever enough to know how to con his nurses, too. All he had to do was get from the hospital to the mansion, pour the stuff in the decanter, return to his bed, then make the phone call that lured Curtis to his death."

"It makes perfect sense, Nan," George said, climbing into the car. "But how do we prove it?"

Nancy didn't answer George right away. She pulled her key from her purse and started the engine, considering George's question. She couldn't believe what she was thinking, but it just might be crazy enough to work.

"I can see a wild plan forming in that brain of yours, Nancy," George commented.

"True," Nancy murmured. "Think of it, George. There's no way to prove Spike's guilt, not after five years. He's got to confess to the crime himself."

"But how can we ever get him to do that?" George asked.

Nancy tightly clutched the steering wheel. "Maybe *we* can't get him to confess," she said, "but I know someone who can—Curtis Taylor himself!"

Chapter

Fourteen

"NANCY, HAVE YOU LOST your mind?" George fixed her brown eyes on Nancy in an uncomprehending stare. "What do you mean, *Curtis* can make Spike confess? I know you don't think Curtis Taylor is coming back from the dead."

"Of course not," Nancy said evenly as she drove down Route 459 back to Maywood. "But I do think we can take advantage of the rumors about his so-called return. After all, Spike never saw Curtis's dead body. There must be some very small part of him that wonders whether those rumors could be true. That's the part we've got to work on."

With a sideways glance at George, Nancy

said, "Remember those Curtis Taylor look-
alikes we saw our first day here?"

George shot Nancy a look of surprise. "You
mean you want one of those guys to pretend to
be the real Curtis?" she guessed. When Nancy
nodded, George leaned back in the passenger
seat, letting out a long breath of air. "I
wouldn't have thought of that idea in a million
years."

"How about a billion?" Nancy teased, grinning. "Now let's head for the other hospital."

The girls reached the center of Maywood
some time later, and Nancy turned onto the
road that would take them to the Maywood
Medical Center. Reaching the visitors' lot,
Nancy spied Louisa's sedan and pulled into a
space as close to it as she could find.

"Wait until Bess and Louisa hear about what
we found out today," George said as she
followed Nancy through the hospital's entrance.

At the reception desk the girls were informed that all visitors to Tyrone Taylor had to
be cleared by his staff. After telling the nurse
their names, the girls waited as she punched in
a number on her phone.

"Miss Marvin?" the nurse said into the
receiver as Nancy and George suppressed a
giggle. "There's a Nancy Drew and a George
Fayne here to see Mr. Taylor."

"I guess Bess is back to being Tyrone's

personal assistant today," George whispered, leaning close to Nancy.

A moment later the nurse hung up and told Nancy and George, "You can go up. It's room four-oh-six."

Just as they stepped out of the elevator on the fourth floor, Bess appeared, waiting to greet them. "Hi, you two," she said warmly. "Tyrone is much better today. Wait until you see. But, Nancy, Louisa and I didn't have much luck with our investigating this morning. None of the crew members we talked to saw anything unusual backstage last night. And no one knew anything about J.J., either."

"It's okay, Bess," Nancy said with a smile. "George and I found out everything we need to know. We'll tell you all about it in Tyrone's room. We want him to hear, too."

Stepping into room 406, Nancy was surprised to see Tyrone looking as well as he did. Although there were a few red patches on his hands and neck, and his face looked slightly pale, the singer looked almost totally healthy. Bess, Louisa, and a guard wearing a Greenwood security uniform were also there.

"Hey," Tyrone greeted them with a weak smile. "How'd you like the show last night? How about that light show?"

"Someone almost turned the lights out on you, Tyrone—for good," Nancy replied, looking concerned.

At that, Tyrone's face darkened. "Yeah, so Bess was telling me. Any luck finding out who?"

Nodding, Nancy said, "I think we've got our man."

"Who? Who is it?" Tyrone asked anxiously, raising himself up on his elbows.

"Spike Wilson," Nancy said levelly.

Tyrone looked at her in surprise, then lay back against the pillows, shaking his head sadly. "But how . . . why?"

Nancy and George quickly recounted their discovery that the song "Melanie" hadn't been written by Curtis, telling the others all they had pieced together about Spike during their conversation with Melanie at the estate.

"Let me get this straight," said Bess, who was leaning against the windowsill. "You think Spike hated Curtis for stealing Melanie away from him." Next to her, Louisa was shaking her head in disbelief.

George nodded. "Right. Even though she and Spike were never really together."

"Unbelievable!" Tyrone exclaimed. "My uncle was so good to him, too." A bitter look came into his eyes. "I'd like to—"

"He's not going to get away with it, Tyrone," Nancy promised. "But I'll need a little help from you in order to nab him."

Tyrone gestured to his hospital bed. "I don't

know how much help I can give," he said apologetically.

As Nancy and George explained their plan, Tyrone raised his eyebrows. "You really think you can get one of those impersonators to convince Spike that he's Uncle Curtis and get Spike to confess?" he asked dubiously.

"That's crazy," Louisa said, but from the smile curving her lips, Nancy could tell she was intrigued by the idea.

"It's our only chance," Nancy told them. She fumbled in her purse until she found the miniature tape recorder she usually kept there. "And if all goes well, we'll even get his confession on tape."

Tyrone looked from Nancy to George, to Bess and Louisa, then shrugged and reached for his address book in the drawer of the hospital room's bedside table. "Norman Rhodes, Marv McCoy, and Jeff Ryan," he told her, flipping open the book to the right page and handing it to Nancy. "You can use this phone by the bed here."

Nancy dialed the first impersonator's number. Norman Rhodes was unavailable due to a prior commitment, according to the message on his phone machine. Marv McCoy lived in St. Louis. He said he could be there in a couple of days, but Nancy didn't have that much time. She crossed her fingers, then dialed the last number, which was local. She hoped Jeff Ryan was her man.

"Hello? Jeff Ryan speaking."

"Jeff, my name is Nancy Drew. I'm calling about a special assignment for today and tonight, impersonating Curtis Taylor. But I have to warn you, there may be some danger involved. What you're doing could help us to catch a murderer."

"Danger is my middle name," Jeff told her. "As long as the price is right."

Nancy rolled her eyes, then quickly checked with Tyrone, who assured her money wouldn't be a problem. Then she made arrangements for Jeff to bring a guitar and meet her and her friends at Louisa's in an hour.

"Jeff does a dynamite imitation of Uncle Curtis," Tyrone said after Nancy had hung up. "He's really good."

"Well, let's hope so," Nancy said, leveling a serious gaze at him. "Because this time he's got to be good enough to fool a killer."

Jeff Ryan got to Louisa's just a few minutes after Nancy and her friends returned from the hospital.

"The first thing we have to do," she told Jeff as they all settled in the living room, "is to teach you this song." She gave him the music to "Melanie" and played the cassette of Tyrone singing it.

"That song stinks," Jeff said bluntly. "Why don't you pick a different number? Curtis had so many good ones. This is a dog."

"I know," Nancy said with a smile, "but it's got to be this one."

Shaking his head in dismay, Jeff Ryan took out his acoustic guitar and set to work as Nancy, Bess, George, and Louisa all listened, pacing around the room. Jeff was a quick study and in less than an hour could sing and play the song well.

Louisa was bringing a plate of cookies into the living room just as he finished playing the song through perfectly. Nancy noticed an almost haunted look come over her face.

"My goodness, he looks and sounds *exactly* like Curtis Taylor," Louisa said.

Next Nancy told Jeff about the case, and about her plan, telling him exactly what to say when he called Spike. There was a hint of skepticism in the actor's blue eyes as he said, "Sounds weird, but if you think it'll help catch a bad guy, I guess I'm game."

A few hours later Nancy announced, "I think we're as ready as we'll ever be to call Spike." She was confident that Jeff knew his lines and that he knew enough to improvise if he needed to. "Okay, get ready everybody," she said.

Nancy dialed Spike's number on the living room phone and handed the receiver to Jeff.

Then she went into the kitchen, where Louisa handed her the extension she'd already picked up. Nancy put it to her ear and listened as the others stood by.

"Hello?" Spike's voice said over the line. A silence, and then again, "Hello?"

"Hello, Spike. Guess who this is?"

Another silence.

"Don't you recognize my voice? You ought to."

"What the—?"

"You tried to kill me, Spike. But you failed. I'm still alive, and now I've come back."

Nancy held her breath, listening. To her, Jeff Ryan's rough voice sounded exactly like Curtis's. But would Spike be able to tell the difference? Would he go for it?

"Whoever you are, you've got a lot of nerve," Spike sputtered angrily. "Why, I ought to just call the—"

"Go ahead. Call the cops, Spike. That'd be just fine. I'm sure they'll be real interested to hear all the gory details."

"You're not Curtis," Spike said, his breathing coming hard. "Curtis is dead."

Nancy heard Jeff Ryan chuckle. "Hey, Spike, the coffin was closed at my funeral, remember? That's just the way I wanted it. I had to disappear for a while. Until I found out who was trying to kill me. And now I know."

Spike's voice was shaky as he asked, "Why should I believe you?"

"Believe this, then." Ryan began to sing softly:

"Oh, Melanie, Melanie, Melanie.
You are the only one for me.
You left me, and now you're with him.
Someday he'll be gone, though,
And your heart I'll win."

There was an incredibly long silence. "Spike?" Jeff Ryan said at last. "Spike? You still there?"

"Where'd you get that song?" Spike gasped.

"You mailed it to Melanie from the hospital, didn't you, Spike?" Jeff Ryan told him. "Only I happened to get the mail that day. I'm the only one who knows that song exists. Except you, of course."

After another silence that seemed to last for hours, Spike said, "What do you want from me?"

"Meet me at midnight, at the gully. You know where I mean. And you'd better be alone, Spike. Understand?"

There was heavy breathing from Spike's end of the line. "I understand," he said, and hung up.

Nancy hung up, too, and ran back into the

living room in triumph. "You did it, Jeff!" she cried.

"Nancy, just one thing," Bess said.

Hearing the concern in her voice, Nancy turned to look at Bess. "What's that?"

Bess's blue eyes flicked nervously at Nancy. "What if Spike Wilson tries to kill Curtis Taylor all over again?"

Chapter

Fifteen

I T'S TOO DANGEROUS to do this on our own," Nancy told the others. Checking her watch, she saw that it was already after six. "I'd better call the police and see if they can back us up."

Twenty minutes later the details were all arranged. "The police are going to meet us at the gully," Nancy said. "They'll be there the whole time, backing us up." With a grin she looked at her friends and Jeff. "Now, I don't know about you guys, but I'm hungry."

After heating up leftover macaroni and cheese in the microwave, the group played cards until it was time to leave. Nancy felt a nervous tingle as she turned her car onto Route 459. I hope this works, she thought to herself. Because if it doesn't, a killer will go free.

When they reached the spot where Curtis had died, Nancy pulled her car off the road and into the shadow of a grove of trees. Turning off the motor and headlights, she said, "Let's walk from here. We'll hide in the gully and take Spike by surprise."

"Where are the police?" Bess asked, looking around nervously.

"It's only eleven-thirty, Bess," Nancy assured her. "They're due at about eleven forty-five. Don't worry, they'll be here."

The group got out of the car and walked, single file, along the side of the highway to the place where the guardrail shone silver in the moonlight. "If we crouch down here in the tall grass on the side of the gully," Nancy pointed out, "he won't be able to see us."

Walking up to Jeff, she took out her miniature tape recorder and dropped it into his jacket pocket. "You know what to do," she told him. "Good luck."

"Thanks," Jeff said. "I'm going to give it everything I've got."

Nancy smiled at him. "Now we just wait until everyone shows up."

"Isn't it midnight yet?" Bess whispered after a half hour had gone by. "Where's Spike?"

Nancy checked her watch by the light of the moon. It was ten after twelve.

"Never mind Spike—where are the police?" Louisa asked anxiously.

Nancy wished she had an answer for her.

"Shhh!" George warned. Looking up, Nancy spied a lone car coming slowly down the highway. It pulled over across the road from the gully. The headlights went out, and Spike Wilson emerged from the car, looking around nervously.

Nancy pounded her fist into her palm. "Rats, he got here before the police," she said in a hoarse whisper. "Now, if they show up, it'll blow the whole show." She let out a frustrated breath. "Oh, well. Here goes nothing. Jeff, you're on."

Jeff got up, walked up to the guardrail, and hopped over it. "Hello, there, old buddy," he called out.

Spike whipped around to face him, and even in the moonlight, through the tall grass, Nancy could see that his face had gone dead white. Jeff looked virtually identical to Curtis Taylor. The impersonator wore a white suit, and his dark hair was styled exactly as the singer had worn his.

Spike backed up against the side of his car, breathing hard. "What the— Curtis? Is that really you?"

"Yep," Jeff said, his voice sounding just like the late star's. "It's me all right."

"Are you alone?" Spike asked nervously.

"Alone—and alive," Jeff retorted.

Spike swiped at his forehead with the back of his hand. "So you—you didn't die that night?" he stammered.

"No, Spike, I didn't. I managed to escape with a few scratches, that's all. A nice old couple came by and picked me up. Foreigners, they were, from Germany. Didn't even know who I was. Since then I've been in hiding. And all that time I've been wondering who did it. Now I know." He took a step forward, to the edge of the highway. "Why'd you do it, Spike?"

Spike's eyes were transfixed on the man who stood across the road from him. "What are you talking about, Curtis?" he stammered.

Ignoring him, Jeff went on. "Sure, I fired you, but that kind of thing happens all the time. Remember, I also gave you your big break. And you would have gotten other jobs if it hadn't been for your accident. You can't rightly blame me for that. So why did you do it? Why did you put those barbiturates in my bourbon? You must have hated me pretty bad to have made that long trip from the hospital just to spike my liquor."

As Nancy watched, a change seemed to come over Spike. He clenched his hands into fists and stepped forward menacingly. "I bet you never knew I was that smart, did you, Curtis?" Spike sneered. "All I had to do was hot-wire a car and drive to Greenwood." He let out a little cackle. "Oh, my leg hurt, all right, but it was worth it."

"But why, Spike?" Jeff pressed.

Nancy noticed Jeff take a slight step backward as Spike advanced on him, clenching and unclenching his fists. *Where are the police?* Nancy's mind screamed.

"Because of Melanie!" Spike bellowed. "Because I loved her. I still love her. I thought she'd come to *me* after you were gone, not to that skunk J.J." His face twisted with fury, Spike went on. "And then she had the nerve to tell me she was still in love with you."

Standing his ground, Jeff said, "So you went and smashed up my tombstone on account of that, didn't you, Spike?"

"So what if I did!"

"And you tried to kill Tyrone, too," Jeff continued.

"He was onto me," Spike snarled. "He hired that girl to spy on me. But I got a peek at her address in Tyrone's book, and I'll get rid of her. The way I'm going to get rid of you—for good."

Nancy heard Louisa gasp beside her. "Nancy, we have to do something," she whispered.

Seeing Jeff Ryan start to back away from

Spike, Nancy stood up, climbed over the guardrail, and ran over.

"You're not going to get rid of anyone, Spike," Nancy said, coming up next to Jeff. A moment later Bess, Louisa, and George came up behind them. "We've got your whole confession down on tape, and the police are on their way. You're going to jail for the murder of Curtis Taylor."

"What—?" Spike sputtered, looking frantically at Jeff Ryan.

The actor held out his hand, saying, "Sorry, but the name's really Jeff Ryan, not Curtis."

Spike started backing up, his eyes darting back and forth. "You little witch," he murmured bitterly. "You tricked me!" His eyes were wild with panic.

Turning on his heel, he yanked open the passenger door of his car, jumped in, and slammed it shut.

Nancy turned to George and shouted, "Quick, my car!" George took off toward the stand of trees where Nancy's car was parked as Spike gunned the engine. With a screech his tires spun on the asphalt.

At last Nancy heard in the distance the comforting wail of a police siren. But in the meantime Spike was getting away.

"Watch out!" Nancy yelled to her friends. She and her party scattered, leaping in all directions to stay clear of Spike's careening car. Spike was still burning rubber as he pulled it around in a sharp U-turn. But the car lost control in midturn, its rear slamming hard against the guardrail, then ricocheting back across the road.

Suddenly there was a loud pop as the left rear tire exploded. The car veered to the left and came to a wobbling stop in the middle of the highway.

Moments later two police cars pulled up. Four officers jumped out, their pistols in hand. "Are you okay?" one of them asked Nancy and her friends while the others approached Spike's car.

"Where were you all this time?" Bess cried.

"Got caught in traffic downtown," the officer explained. "All those tourists."

Nancy, Bess, Louisa, George, and Jeff Ryan watched as the officers handcuffed Spike. "I guess from here Spike can take his chances in court," George murmured.

"Not much of a chance, I'd say," Bess remarked.

"True," Nancy agreed. "But it's a much better chance than he gave Curtis Taylor."

The next night Nancy and her friends stood backstage at the Civic Center, watching the greatest live performance they had ever seen.

In the soft glow of a rose-colored spotlight Melanie had just finished her heart-stopping rendition of "Losin' My Heart." Tears filled Bess's and Louisa's eyes, and Nancy noticed that even George was swallowing hard. When the singer wailed her final note, there was a second of total silence before a tidal wave of applause and cheering filled the hall.

In the middle of it Melanie lifted her slender arms. "Tyrone Taylor," she said loudly, "get on out here!"

Wild cheering and a standing ovation met Tyrone, who ambled onstage, a new neon guitar in hand. He was smiling and looked completely recovered, except for a small bandage on his neck.

After Melanie had signaled for the audience to settle down, she said, "My nephew and I have a little surprise for you."

Tyrone leaned into the mike, adding, "You know we've had a little excitement around here this past week, but it's over now. So Melanie and I wrote a song to express our gratitude to someone very special—someone who helped us out when we needed it the most."

"What's this all about?" George said, craning her neck to get a better look at the stage.

"Beats me," Nancy said.

The band started up a country waltz featuring a fiddle solo, as Tyrone and Melanie put their heads close together and sang:

"Nancy Drew, Nancy Drew,
We're so grateful to you-oo. . . .

"Oh, no!" Nancy cried, covering her face with her hands.

"Smart as a whip, with a heart so true,
Tell me now, what would we do—
Without youuuu—Nancy Drew."

"I don't believe this," Nancy murmured, peeking out of her fingers and shaking her head in embarrassment.

"If you need a clue
Go ask Nancy Drew!"

"Well, that sounds like a gold record to me," Louisa said, squeezing Nancy's shoulder with a laugh. "Just like you, Nancy—pure gold!"

Nancy's next case:

College freshman Ava Woods turned to Campus Connections in hopes of finding her dream date but found herself in the middle of a nightmare instead. Nancy and Bess pose as transfer students to see if they can learn the truth behind her disappearance—and uncover evidence of a chilling criminal conspiracy.

Bess has concocted the perfect plan: date every guy on the Campus Connections list. But when the main man behind the dating service turns up dead, Nancy has to turn up the heat. Not only is Ava missing—Nancy is now the number-one suspect in a case of murder . . . in *TALL, DARK AND DEADLY*, Case #66 in The Nancy Drew Files™.